Discoverers

Philip Hawthorn

Scripture Union
130 City Road, London EC1V 2NJ.

For Adam Styles, my godson

First published 1990

ISBN 0 86201 618 5

Phototypeset by Input Typesetting Ltd, London
Printed and bound in Great Britain by Cox and Wyman Ltd, Reading

Contents

The Prologue (or 'Bit at the Beginning')

Inside St Margaret's Church in East Hanworth, which is just underneath and to the left of London, lots of people were busily getting ready for the morning service. But along a back corridor, a large monster was peeping out from behind an ever-so-slightly open door. All sixteen of its eyes were wide and unblinking – there was a deathly hush. On the outside of the door was a large notice saying:

Discoverers

9–11 years

OK, it wasn't really a monster. It was the eight members of the group called, obviously, 'Discoverers'. Reverend Wibble, the vicar of St Margaret's, sometimes thought they *were* all monsters, but this morning he was feeling a little more friendly than normal. If you want to know the reason why, you only have to be on the other side of that door . . .

To begin at the beginning . . .

Sunday 4th November

'Quick, he's coming!'

The door around which the group had been crowding was slammed shut, and there was a mad scramble of feet, elbows and chairs. By the time the door handle began to turn, all eight of them were sitting at their tables, staring at the slowly opening door. They all knew that the first person to enter the room would be Reverend Wibble, but it was the person behind him in whom they were really interested. This would be their new group leader, the person with whom they would have to spend sixty minutes every Sunday morning.

Their last leader had left two weeks ago, and they were still sad. Miss Goodman had been dead brill, but not because she had taught them anything dead brill (although she had always wanted to). It was because she had done a deal with them. They would pay attention to her lessons, if she would let them play a game each week. The game had to be first – oh well, she'd thought, at least it got them there on time.

So, they'd played indoor hockey, basketball, a version of rounders (using a rolled up newspaper as a bat and a screwed up one as a ball), Subbuteo, Trivial Pursuit, Scalextric – you name it. The problem was, by the time they had packed up the game there was only about ten minutes left for the lesson. Actually, this wasn't a problem at all to the Discoverers.

So Miss Goodman had turned Sundays from solid boredom into something to be looked forward to. When she had walked out for the last time, it was as though a huge shadow had been cast over St Margaret's. They were sure their new leader would bring back the boredom, and now he (for experience had taught them that men were always the worst) was going to walk through that same door which, two weeks before, had swallowed up Miss Goodman.

Reverend Wibble walked in, followed by an old man. 'Why has he brought his dad with him?' said Deborah to Joel.

'The new leader must be coming next week,' said Adam to Jodi. Reverend Wibble coughed loudly. The group stopped staring at the old man and looked instead at the vicar.

'Good morning, Discoverers,' he said.

'Good mor-ning Rev-rend Wib-ble,' they chanted with one voice, well almost. Reverend Wibble then began to speak, and he had an odd habit of emphasising certain words by opening his eyes wide and thrusting his head forward with a wobble. 'Now you may remember, sadly Miss Goodman has *left* us.' How could they forget? 'This morning, I would like to intro*duce* you to your new leader, Mr Or*lando*.'

Slowly, all eyes moved back from Reverend Wibble to the small man standing next to him. And as their eyes moved, their hearts sank. He was fairly old, fairly round and fairly bald. The Discoverers didn't get as far as noticing that his eyes were bright, and full of life.

'Now, we're all very *grateful* to Mr Orlando for stepping into Miss Goodman's shoes at such short *notice* . . . .'

'They'd be too small for him,' giggled Rachel to Susan, able to spot a joke at fifty paces.

'He'll be with you until the end of the *year*, and I'm sure you'll all appreciate having him as your *leader*.' There was a heavy silence. 'Won't you?'

'Yes,' they said, dutifully, all thinking quite the opposite.

'Now, until Mr Orlando has settled *in*, you'd better get on with some *work*. You can colour the pictures on these sheets of *paper*.' He handed them out one by one, each one taken by a reluctant hand. Then he left, thinking that he would rather be anyone in the world than Mr Orlando at that moment. The Discoverers had really loved Miss Goodman.

They met every week except the last Sunday of the month, which was 'family service' in church. They were all supposed to attend, but only the ones whose parents went to church actually did. It definitely wasn't their favourite event in all the world. Recently, they had got a new curate called Nick who had a puppet called Adrian (whom he called 'Visual Ade'). He appeared during the services and made comments about various people taking part. He also told jokes, but even that was not half as good as playing games with Miss Goodman.

Mr Orlando surveyed his new, colouring group – well, the tops of their heads anyway. Then he slowly sat down on his chair in front of a pale green wall which was covered in various drawings, mainly of men with beards. On the wall opposite was an old faded picture of Jesus carrying a lamb. The other walls contained a few scraps of paper on which had once been written words from the Bible that they had had to remember, called memory verses. They were now forgotten. Hanging from the ceiling were a couple of lop-sided mobiles made out of straws and pipe cleaners.

Suddenly there was the noise of a pencil lead breaking, a sort of 'thd!'

'Oh, Stephen!' Deborah's voice was cross.

'It was an accident,' protested Stephen, still holding Deborah's pencil, the blue lead sitting awkwardly in a crater of shattered wood. 'Sorry, Deborah, I can't help it if I forgot my pencils.' He picked up another one and started to colour again.

Mr Orlando looked slowly around the room. Reverend Wibble had told him about the group members on their slow walk to the room. He now had no problem putting names to people.

There was a trendy-looking boy with gelled fair hair

and a multi-coloured track suit with 'Muddy Fox' on the arms. That must be Adam. He was whispering and giggling with a lively-faced black girl who looked older than eleven – probably Jodi.

Then a boy with fairly thick glasses, head resting on one side, tongue sticking out, experimenting with giving Jesus a blue beard – Joel.

And that must be Susan – tall and slim with a pony tail longer than a real pony's tail – and an open, friendly face.

She sat next to Rachel, her younger sister, who looked like a smaller, more solid version of Susan only with an impish face and freckles.

Next was a boy dressed in smart clothes, constantly shooting glances around the room. This was Wesley. Whenever he caught Mr Orlando's eye, he smiled too nicely and returned to his work.

Then came Deborah, who wore grubby clothes, and had the most bitten fingernails you could imagine. She was still red after her argument with Stephen.

Stephen was rather large with straight hair, glasses and a warm face. He was now shading in the sea with such ferocity that it looked like at any moment there would be another . . .

'Thd!'

'Right, you've had it now,' and Deborah began hitting Stephen, who was holding another broken pencil. The rest of the group looked at the flying fists, and Stephen's efforts to protect his head. He had two younger sisters, and had long ago learned that it was better to hide than strike back and get told off for 'hitting a girl', even though *this* girl could hit twice as hard as him. Then they looked at their new leader. Most of them were old enough to realise that it was a very difficult situation for him – and most of them were secretly pleased.

Mr Orlando just sat there for a second, then simply said, 'Deborah'.

Jodi whispered to Adam, 'How did he know her

name?'

Deborah stopped immediately and looked at Mr Orlando. 'Why are you hitting Stephen?'

'Because he's busted another one of my pencils, that's why.'

'Are you sorry, Stephen?' said Mr Orlando.

'Yes,' was the reply.

'Good. Do you have a pencil sharpener?'

'Yes.'

'Good. Then you can sharpen the pencil for Deborah, and we'll hear no more about it.'

'But that's the fourth pencil he's busted,' protested Deborah, not prepared to see Stephen get off so lightly, 'He's so clumsy and fat and stupid.'

There was an audible gasp from the others.

'Now, Deborah,' said Mr Orlando, 'please tell Stephen you forgive him.'

There was a long pause. Deborah's temper had a fuse as short as a tadpole's tongue, and now her disappointment at their new leader ignited it.

'Deborah?'

'No, I won't – he's broken one pencil too many – and I hate this stinking place, it's stupid – and the Bible's a stupid old book and, why can't we play hockey and, and –,'

She stopped. The others stared. Mr Orlando sat – and didn't look at all the way they'd have expected a grown up who'd been spoken to like *that* to look. When he spoke, it was softly.

'Well, this place may smell a bit, and it may well be stupid, but I'll tell you one thing – the Bible isn't.'

'Yes it is – and boring,' yelled Deborah.

'Really? Well, let me see now . . .' His face became full of far away thoughts. The Discoverers watched, their interest aroused. Suddenly Mr Orlando slammed his hand down on his table.

'Rrrright!' he said with a long 'R' that sounded like a drum roll. Everyone jumped ten centimetres – except for Stephen who, being rather large, managed only five.

'A story. Who wants one!' Silence. 'Well!' said the old man with far more energy than anyone could have imagined. Hands were raised, slowly at first, then more quickly as no-one wanted to be the odd one out. Soon all hands were up – except for one. 'You don't want a story, Deborah?'

'No.'

'Oh, that's a pity, because you're in it,' said Mr Orlando in a matter-of-fact way.

'Really?' said Deborah.

'Yes, and if you don't want the story, then I'm afraid nobody can have it.' The others quickly let Deborah know what they felt about this.

After a short time, Deborah said: 'All right, we'll have the story!' and Susan, Adam, Jodi and Joel climbed off her.

Deborah sharpens up on forgiveness

Still 4th November

The Discoverers sat looking at Mr Orlando. Although the room was silent, the atmosphere was full of the events of the last few minutes.

'Now then,' he began, 'what shall this story be about?'

'I thought you already knew,' said Deborah.

'I know some of it, but I want it to be your story too. Stephen – what's your favourite place?'

Stephen needed only a quarter of a second to think.

'A burger bar.' The others laughed, knowing how true this was. 'Right then, this story takes place in – Stephen's Burger Joint.'

They all laughed, except for Stephen who beamed with pride. It wasn't often he was the centre of attention for something good.

'He had opened the shop all by himself. Soon he invented something that was so popular, the queue to buy it would often reach right along the High Street to the public toilets – sometimes even into them.'

The Discoverers looked at each other. Half of them were wondering what the invention could be. The other half were trying to remember if any grown up had ever talked about public toilets in church before.

'Now,' Mr Orlando continued, 'he called his invention, the Megarooney-Burger.'

'What was in it?' asked Rachel.

'You tell me,' was the reply.

'A massive pure beefburger,' said Susan.

'Two!' added Stephen.

'Really thick cheese,' said Deborah.

'Loads of sweetcorn relish,' said Jodi.

'Juicy tomatoes,' said Joel.

Then came a rush of mouth-slurping ingredients:

'Sliced pickled onions – fried egg – bacon – tomato sauce – lettuce – cucumber – crisps.'

'All of those things,' said Mr Orlando smiling, which was difficult as his mouth was watering so much. 'But the thing that made them absolutely *irresistible*, was the special ingredient . . .'

'Garlic mushrooms!' exclaimed Stephen, dreamily – and you could almost see them in his eyes.

'Rrrright!' said Mr Orlando. 'So you can understand why the invention was so popular. Once people had learned how to eat them without dropping bits all over the place, they counted the seconds till their next one.

'Stephen was rushed off his feet. So he decided to take on an assistant who, I warn you, turns out to be a bit of a sneaky.'

'Go on, Wez,' said Deborah, 'suits you.'

'It couldn't be him, he only eats rice and chocolate biscuits,' said Adam, and they laughed. Wez would have felt cross if it hadn't been more or less true.

'I'll be him,' continued Adam.

'Good on you! Don't worry, Wez, your turn will come. Adam, the new assistant, was a dream come true for Stephen.' Adam put both his thumbs up, nodded his head and said coolly, 'All right'.

'He was eager to do well at his job. He learned how to make Megarooney-Burgers in no time, and soon he could make them faster than his boss. He couldn't have been more helpful. He stayed late every night to clear up, and as soon as he was trusted with the key to the shop, he was in every morning getting things ready for the day. Stephen was very pleased.

'After a few months, Adam had got so fast that Stephen put him in charge of the shop, while he worked in the office at the back, looking after the business. He thought Adam would object to so much extra work, so he sometimes came out to offer help. But Adam seemed only too pleased to be in the shop alone and hurriedly sent Stephen back to his office, out of sight. Once or twice Stephen worried about this; it was almost as if Adam didn't want him around. But soon, any worries he had about Adam were forgotten as the burgers went through the roof!'

'Did the grill blow up?' said Rachel with a giggle.

'No, stupid,' said Wez, thankful for a chance to show Mr Orlando something he knew. 'It means the sales figures were very good – it's a business expression, isn't it, Mr Orlando?'

'Yes, sort of,' he said, still laughing at Rachel's joke.

'Things were going very well, although Stephen did think it odd that despite them getting through more burgers than ever before, the amount of money they made didn't seem to go up as much as he expected.

'Soon, Stephen decided that Adam needed an assistant. When he was told, Adam got quite cross and said that he could manage alone. But Stephen insisted.

"After all," he said, "you can't move so fast since you put on that extra weight." So, in no time at all, a junior burger-maker appeared on the scene.'

Hands shot up faster than rockets on Bonfire Night.

'Thank you for offering,' said Mr Orlando, 'but this is Deborah's story. The new assistant was called Deborah.' Deborah was glad she'd let the story go on.

'Deborah arrived for her first day's work.

"Now, you know you finish at seven o'clock tonight, don't you?" said Stephen.

"Oh," said Deborah, "I thought it was five, that's when I told my mum to pick me up." Stephen thought for a minute.

"Well you'd better phone your mum and tell her.

"But I haven't got any money."

"Oh, Adam will lend you some, won't you, Adam?" Adam scowled, and fished out ten pence. "Adam will start to train you as soon as you've done." So Deborah phoned her mum, and Stephen went back to his office.

'Now, during the next month, Adam became very

crosspatchy, so much so that Stephen became almost scared to go into the shop. He's probably worried about his weight problem, he thought. He seems to get fatter every day. I wonder why?

'So Stephen spent most of his time in his office, and for this reason, he hadn't really seen Deborah since her first day. Then one Thursday morning, there was a tap on the door.'

'I thought you only got taps on sinks,' quipped Rachel.

'Ssshh!' said the others.

' "Come in," said Stephen in his most important voice, in case it was a television reporter who had come to make a film about his brilliant success. The door opened, and in walked Deborah. "What can I do for you, young feller-me-lad?" He'd always wanted to call someone that, and saw no reason why her being a girl should stop him.

"Sir," began Deborah., "I don't mean to be impatient, but when will I learn to make burgers?"

"What?" said Stephen, "I thought Adam had taught you ages ago." Deborah looked at the floor, and drew circles on the carpet with her right foot.

"I don't mean to tell tales, but he makes me stay in the big deep-freeze most of the day, counting burgers and buns. Sometimes I get icicles on my nose. The only time I go into the shop is to clear up when he's finished."

Stephen suddenly looked straight at Deborah. "When you are counting burgers, do you notice anything strange?" Deborah thought, and then said, "Only that, when I count them in the morning, there don't seem to be as many as the night before." '

Mr Orlando slammed his hand down on the table, like he had before. They all jumped twice as far.

' "Just as I suspected!" said Stephen. "Send Adam in to me." ' A tingle of excitement ran round the room.

'Adam came into the office with the usual scowl on his face. He couldn't sit down as none of the chairs was strong enough to take his weight. "I've just been doing the accounts, Adam. Over the past few months, lots of burgers have gone missing – and I know where they are."

"Where?" said Adam.

'Stephen pointed to Adam's enormous stomach. "There! I've worked out that in the last three months you've eaten over five hundred burgers – without paying for a single one of them. You're as guilty as a grinning cat sitting next to an empty goldfish bowl. And you will have to pay me back every penny – you rotten burger burgler!"

'Adam fell to his knees with an enormous thud and tummy-wobble – the earth thought it had had a quake without realising.

"Oh, please spare me, Stephen . . . sir! I didn't mean to, they were so lovely, I couldn't resist them . . . it's because you are such a genius to invent the Megarooney-Burger, sir – you are the Boris Becker of fast food, sir – I only ate them to show you how much I respect your burger-brilliance, oh-oh-ooohhh!" And Adam collapsed in tears and grease on the floor.

'Stephen looked down on him and smiled. Yes I am pretty brilliant, he thought. "All right, I'll let you off this time. But never gobble another freebie burger in my shop, understand?" Adam looked up at his boss.

"Oh thank you, sir, thank you, you are so kind – so kind." There was a slight pause, then Adam added, "– er, would you do me one more favour, sir?"

"What?" said Stephen.

"Help me up." Stephen did so, and watched him squeeze out of the door. As soon as it was shut behind him, Adam's face turned into a slimy smile.

"Oh, and Adam," shouted Stephen. Adam turned back into a humble, sorry lump and opened the door again.

"Yes, sir?"

"Teach Deborah how to make burgers. She said she

hasn't learned yet."

'Adam closed the door and straightened up again, but this time his face was a sneer. So, that little creep has been blabbing about me has she. I'll show her. "Oh Deb-or-ah!" he sang.

'Deborah came, and said excitedly, "Are you going to teach me how to make Megaroonies?"

"No, grease-face," sneered Adam. "I'm going to teach you a lesson. Remember that ten pence I lent you when you first came here?" Deborah nodded. "Well you never gave it me back – and I want it now!"

"B-b-but you know I never have any money on me," said Deborah.

"In that case," yelled Adam, "you're fired – *and* I'm going to ring the police and report you as a thief!"

"Oh, please," pleaded Deborah, "I'll pay you back tomorrow, really I will – I need this job, it's the only one I've got, you can't give me the sack, please!"

'But Adam had already called the police. Soon the sound of a siren, like an electronic owl, could be heard getting nearer and nearer – and eventually a police car screeched to a halt outside the shop. Two police officers rushed in.

"Evenin' all," said one.

"Don't worry about that, where's the thief?" said the other, handcuffs at the ready.

'Adam opened his mouth ready to speak . . .'

But before Mr Orlando could continue, he was interrupted by the real Deborah, 'It's not fair!'

'Oh?' said Mr Orlando.

'Adam has been let off loads of money, he should forgive Deborah a measly ten pence.'

Mr Orlando smiled and continued, 'Well, listen Deborah. Before Adam could say anything, a voice from behind them said, "*There's* the thief!" It was Stephen, and he was pointing straight at Adam.

"Right you are, sir," said one of the officers, and snapped the handcuffs on to Adam's wrists quicker than you could say "griddled wombat". Stephen looked at Adam.

"I forgave you everything you owed me, and you couldn't even let Deborah off ten pence. You can go to jail, where you belong. If you're lucky, they'll let you have a job in the kitchen."

"Reckon they'll have a big enough cell for him?" said the first police officer.

"They'll have to knock two together," said the other. And they left with one criminal, and two Megarooney-burgers. The end.'

The Discoverers cheered.

'Thanks for your help – nine heads are better than one,' said Mr Orlando.

'That was brill,' said Joel.

'Glad you liked it, actually it's from the Bible.'

'They didn't have burgers in the Bible – did they?' asked Rachel, ready to go and check.

'No, I changed the characters, and brought it a bit more up to date, but the story's the same. See, not so boring, eh, Deborah?'

Deborah looked down and smiled. 'No.'

'Now tell me, do you ever do things that you ask God to forgive you for?'

Deborah thought, uncertain what this latest question was leading to. She decided to be honest, 'Course I do.'

'And does he forgive you?'

'Yeah – when I say sorry.'

'How many times do you think God has forgiven you in your life?'

Deborah thought. 'Lots,' she said.

'More times than you have hairs on your head,' said Mr Orlando. Then he continued. 'It's not fair, is it?'

'What isn't?' Deborah asked.

'Well, it's like in the story. You've been forgiven lots, and you won't even forgive Stephen for breaking one pencil.' Deborah looked down again.

'You see, everyone, God is fair. If we forgive people,

he forgives us. Rrrright,' Mr Orlando slapped the table, 'ten minutes left, back to your colouring.' All heads bowed, except for Stephen's. He was still without any pencils. After a minute or so, Deborah, still with her head down, whispered to Stephen, 'It's OK about my pencil,' then quietly rolled a newly sharpened red over to him. Stephen's podgy fingers picked it up, and carefully, very carefully, began to colour.

Deborah looked up and caught Mr Orlando's eye. The look in it made Deborah go sort of melty – it was as if God himself was saying, 'Well done, Deborah.' Meanwhile, the others realised they were nearly at the end of the lesson – and they hadn't once thought about a game.

Adam discovers a different goal

Sunday 11th November

Adam woke up. He opened his eyes and looked at the wall. It was covered in photographs, posters, charts and a map of the world. Everything was red and white, and bore the name 'Liverpool' (even though he had been born in Brighton). He humphed over on to his other side and saw his desk, covered in recent attempts to make his sister Abigail a birthday card. In front of the desk was his Lego. David, the youngest in the family, had been playing with it and had made a dinosaur, or a castle – or was it a space rocket? Anyway, whatever it was, it had lots of unused pieces lying around it. This had made Adam's midnight trip to the kitchen for a drink a very painful experience – like walking barefoot and blindfold over a pebbly beach.

Then his eyes came to rest on his red football kit. Normally at this time on a Sunday it was brown, and spinning at great speed along with the rest of the week-end wash. But today it was clean and carefully ironed, waiting to be worn. The door opened and his father strode in, smiling all over his bearded face.

'Here's a mug of tea for the *star* player.' He looked for a space on Adam's bedside table and finding none, placed it on top of Adam's Bible. 'Ha, you won't be needing that this morning, will you? Don't lie in for too long, Adam, we've got to be there in good time so you can get used to the pitch. Just think, my son in the semi-final of the under-11s district cup – what a star – I wish your grandfather was still alive to see it.' He flicked a Lego brick into the air with his foot and headed it into the wastepaper bin. 'Ye-e-e-s!' he shouted, 'Barnes gets his second.' With that he breezed out of the room, and soon Adam could hear him rough-and-tumbling with David and Abigail.

Adam got up, washed, dressed and opened the curtains. The rain which had forced yesterday's match to be moved to today had now stopped. The kick-off was at eleven forty-five, the same time that Discoverers finished. He would have to miss it if he wanted to get to the match on time.

Adam didn't mind. He was not a regular Discoverer – although he had been most weeks since the games were introduced, because he won most of them. He liked being the best at things; it was cool. He picked up his mug of tea, but it had stuck to the Bible which made him spill it. As he was mopping the crinkling pages he read the writing on the inside of the cover, 'To Adam – the star of the holiday club – Nick'. He had been given it at Easter when he'd been to the holiday club at St Margaret's. He'd said he wanted to 'follow Jesus' at the time, but only because his friend Jodi had. He looked at Nick's signature, then at something written after it that he'd never noticed before: 'Matthew 5:16'. Although he didn't often read his Bible, he knew that this was a verse in the book of Matthew. He looked it up. It said: 'Let your light shine before people . . .'

He was packing his bag when he remembered Mr Orlando. He paused, and then for some unexplainable reason he felt he ought to go to Discoverers, to the beginning at least. He finished packing his bag, ate a quick breakfast and headed for the front door.

'Where are you off to? You don't need to leave this early,' said his father with his mouth half full of toast.

'I'm, er, well, I . . .'

'You're not going to church, are you? Listen my lad – you're the star of that team. They need you more than a bunch of do-gooders.'

'I'm just going to tell them I won't be coming, that's all,' he said.

'Well, make sure you do – you've worked had for this.

Don't throw it away.'

Adam set off. St Margaret's was in the opposite direction from the playing fields, so he'd have to be quick. On his way he met Roger Frewin, who was his twin striker. They had been good friends, but not since Roger had joined his older brother's gang, the Recreation Street Wreckers.

'All right?' said Roger.

'All right?' replied Adam.

'Ain't you going the wrong way?'

'I'm, er, just going to see someone first.'

'Make sure you're on time – me and the others are depending on you. We're gonna thrash those Rovers.'

'OK, see you,' and Adam hurried on.

Meanwhile, at St Margaret's the Discoverers had arrived to find the door of their room locked. They had questioned Reverend Wibble about this, but he had no idea what Mr Orlando was up to inside either. Eventually, at ten forty-five on the dot, there was a scrabbling sound from the other side, followed by the click of the key being turned in the lock. The door opened and Mr Orlando peeped out.

'Come in, come in!' He opened the door and they filed in.

At first they thought they had somehow got the room mixed up with another one. They hardly recognised it. The walls had the same familiar paintings and things, but the tables – rather than being in rows, were arranged in a circle.

'Sit anywhere,' said Mr Orlando excitedly as he placed a saucer in front of each place. When they had each sat down, there were two places left.

'Good, just one place left for Adam.'

'But,' began Joel, 'there's another one as well.'

'Yes, that's for me,' said Mr Orlando, and proved it by sitting down.

Jodi spoke: 'The leader sitting with us?'

'Looks like it, doesn't it? Anyway, I'm not just a leader, I'm a learner too.'

'Who do you learn from?' asked Rachel.

'Oh, from God, from you lot, from everyone – you're never too old to be taught a thing or two.' They would have stared at each other longer if Adam hadn't walked in at that moment. He hardly noticed the rearranged tables.

'Oh, Adam, thought we'd lost you – come and sit down. Oh dear, you get the booby prize – a seat next to me!'

Adam sat down, trying to keep the bag he was carrying out of sight and still look cool. He opened his mouth to speak, then thought he'd wait for the right moment.

'Now, then,' continued Mr Orlando, 'you all like games, don't you?' They nodded. 'Well, in that case we'll have one a bit later on.' They couldn't believe it – not even after last week. 'On one condition,' continued Mr Orlando. Here it comes, they thought. 'That I'm allowed to join in.'

Before they could say anything, Mr Orlando continued. 'Rrright! Discoverers of the Round Table, tell me something: What have you discovered?'

'About what?' asked Susan after a pause in which the others had thought the same question.

'About Jesus.' Another silence.

'He's got a beard,' suggested Deborah.

'He's, er, the Son of God,' said Joel. There then followed a string of other things they remembered from the Bible or songs.

Finally, Wez added, looking at Adam, 'He gets cross if we miss church on Sunday.'

'Hmm,' said Mr Orlando thoughtfully, not agreeing or disagreeing. He took out a bag, and from it produced eight small white objects shaped like tablets. He placed one on each saucer, then took out a box of matches. Lighting a match, he went round and lit the top of each one. Before he had got to the last one, the first to have been lit started to fizz, and enormous snake-like creatures started to emerge from the top of the tablet. Even though the tablets were small, the snakes were enormous. They were over an inch wide, and seemed to wriggle and squirm on for ever. The Discoverers watched in amazement.

Eventually they all finished, and the Discoverers sat staring at the eight snakes.

'Indoor Chinese fireworks,' Mr Orlando said. 'Couldn't let Bonfire Night pass like a damp squib. Amazing what can happen from one small light. Now before I tell you what *I've* discovered about Jesus, let's sing. Everyone know "Give me oil in my lamp, keep me burning"?' They knew it and groaned. He opened a guitar case in the corner, brought out a shiny black guitar, and started playing – a reggae rhythm. They all sang, and even quite enjoyed it – especially Jodi.

Adam, who was good at singing, was getting edgy. He had meant just to announce his departure and go. Then he had decided to stay, for a bit, anyway. Now the thought of his father's temper and his team-mates' disappointment was starting to eat away at him. What should he do? But finding an answer was like searching for a black cat in a dark room.

'What does it mean, "Give me oil in my lamp"?' said Mr Orlando. They'd never thought about a song really *meaning* anything before. 'I suppose nowadays it ought to be "give me rechargeable batteries in my torch". No idea? Well, why do the ushers in cinemas have a light?'

'To show people where to go,' said Rachel who had been last night to see *Mary Poppins II*.

'Good,' said Mr Orlando. '*We* can show people the right way, too. We haven't got real lights of course, but it's like . . . well if you have a difficult decision and don't know what to do, you say "I'm in the dark" don't you? Then when something helps you, you say "that's thrown some light on the problem" – or something. Well Jesus wants us to show people the best way to live – we are his lights! See?"

'But how do we show people?' asked Susan.

'We live the way Jesus wants us to – the best way, the most exciting way.'

'And how do we know what that is?' asked Joel.

'By following him – that's the way to let your light shine. Ah, now there's a verse about that, anyone know where that is?'

Everyone shook their head, except for Wez who was looking in his Bible, and Adam who said, 'Matthew chapter five.'

'Good, Adam,' said Mr Orlando.

'But if we have lights, they have to be switched on, though,' said Rachel.

'Ex-actly!' enthused Mr Orlando. 'But being a Christian's all about being switched on. It's not for wimps! It's brrrrrill.'

They laughed.

'Surprised?' he added. They nodded.

'I've discovered that Jesus is full of surprises – always was, always will be. Every story about him or by him. You see Jesus turned things downside up, outside in and bout around. If you thought you had him all sewn up, he'd take your ideas and unstitch them.

'OK – everyone, look in the gospels and find a time when Jesus surprised someone – then write about it, or draw a picture or something – and make sure it's got lots of colours. This room needs a bit of brightening up.'

They all opened their Bibles and began searching – no-one had ever used the words 'Jesus' and 'surprise' in the same sentence before.

Adam looked dumbstruck. He didn't know what to do – this was all new to him. Could it be that he was enjoying church, and they weren't even playing a game? He looked up and saw that Mr Orlando was looking at him too.

'What's up?' he said.

'Nothing,' said Adam, and looked away.

'Shall I tell you another surprise about Jesus? If you shine for him, he'll never – *never* let you down. It's like we're all in his team together – only *all* of us are stars – oh, that's great, do you get it – we shine like stars?'

But this was too much for Adam, who rushed out of the room. 'Well *I* thought it was funny. Come on you rabble – get on,' said Mr Orlando with a cheeky smile, 'I'm just going for a walk.' And he left, too.

Outside, Adam stomped down the corridor towards the door. Why shouldn't he play football? He could leave Discoverers anyway – stupid snakes, stupid stuff – oh rats! He stopped, realising he had forgotten to pick up his bag. He couldn't go back in after leaving like that. He stood facing the wall, then he put his head against it, not knowing what to do. At this moment, Mr Orlando reached him.

Adam told him about the postponed football match, about his dad, everything. After he'd finished, Mr Orlando said, 'Well, Adam, what's more important, football or Jesus?' Adam had expected this question.

'I thought it was football – but I guess it ought to be following Jesus.'

'No "ought" about it – do you *want* to? Jesus wouldn't want you to because you had to.'

'Yes. Yes, I think it is.' And Adam turned to go back into the room.

Mr Orlando stopped him by gently pushing his bag into his stomach. 'I think you forgot this.' Adam looked up, surprised. 'If it was every week, you might have a tough choice. But as for today – it's not your fault it's been rearranged, and it wouldn't do for your team to be without their *star* player in a semi-final, would it? Can't let the side down. Anyway, Jesus wants us to shine at what we're good at – he actually enjoys seeing us have fun – go on, you'll make the kick-off if you run. See you later – it's a shame you'll miss the rest of the session though, we're going to play four-a-side football.'

Adam smiled, then rushed off. He was in too much

of a spin to wonder what Mr Orlando had meant by 'see you later'. However, he soon found out. It was during the second half of the game that he noticed him on the touchline, cheering like mad, along with Adam's dad and a few others. It made Adam feel like a *real* superstar.

Adam scored two goals, but the Rovers won 3–2. As he was walking off the field, Roger came up to him.

'Stupid ref. We should have won that, eh Ads?' Adam nodded.

In the changing room afterwards the man who ran the team, Mr Armstrong, gave his after-match talk.

'Now lads, you played well – but at the end of the day it's about who scores the most goals – and today, they did. Anyway, I've decided that from now on, we're going to play all our matches on Sundays – kick-off eleven o'clock. OK, see you then.'

Adam went hot and cold. What should he do? If the decision was hard, telling Mr Armstrong would be even harder.

'You all right, Adam?' It was Mr Armstrong.

Adam, caught off guard, said, 'I can't play on Sundays.' Everyone stopped and looked at him.

Roger Frewin said, 'What you on about? You've got to –'

'Why not?' said Mr Armstrong. Adam's courage left him.

'I've, er, got to help my dad.'

'Every week?' Adam looked at the ground, and nodded.

'Right. Well, Roger, we'll have to find you another striking partner.' And they left it there. Adam was pleased he'd made the decision, but felt awful that he'd told a lie – he hoped Jesus would understand.

Outside, he was walking towards his dad's car, when another man approached him.

'Hello, son – I'm Mr MacDonald, I run the Rovers. I thought your team played really well. Sorry you had to lose.'

'I haven't got a team,' said Adam. It was now beginning to sink in, and it hurt a bit.

'Oh?' said Mr MacDonald, taken aback, 'Why's that, then?'

'Because . . . just because.'

'Oh, well, you could join us if you like. The final's in three weeks time.'

'Do you play your matches on Saturdays?'

'Oh yes, some teams have started playing on Sundays, but I don't want to – you see I teach at church normally. We're training here on Wednesday – come along if you want to.' And he left.

Adam could have burst with joy. He started to run towards his dad's car, remembering Mr Orlando's words about Jesus not letting him down.

Susan cares for the world

Sunday 18th November

It was a beautiful, sunny day. A day when autumn had put up a fight as if to say, 'Hang on, winter, I'm not quite finished yet.' The air was as crisp and clean as the delicate frost which covered everything like a layer of sifted sugar. The sky was the palest of blues, and the watery sun was more radiant with brightness than heat, which it was saving for next summer.

Susan walked along the main road to Discoverers with a piece of paper in her hand. She had had a school project hanging over her all week, but had put it off and put it off – and now she was panicking. Her whole class was doing the project, called *Caring for the World*, and her group had to do an assembly. She had to have an idea for it by tomorrow. The rest of the day she would have to spend being polite at her grandma's. Her only chance was to try and do some work on it during Discoverers and hope that Mr Orlando wouldn't notice.

'Rrrright,' came the familiar word, accompanied by the usual slap on the table, 'we'll stop there.' They had been playing table tennis in doubles. Jodi and Adam had won. Wez (who had been paired with Stephen), was not pleased.

They settled into their circle. This being their third week, they were looking forward to the lesson because they knew that almost anything could happen. Even Mr Orlando probably didn't know exactly how much they would all discover today. 'Now, as you know, next Sunday is the 24th, the last one of the month.'

'What about the 31st?' put in Stephen.

'November only has thirty days, you dumbo,' sneered Wez, glad to be in with a fact to impress Mr Orlando.

Mr Orlando paused, then carried on, 'Anyway, the point is, next Sunday is family service.' The group let out a groan. 'Come on, it's not the end of the world. What's wrong with family services?'

'Every time all the grown-ups stand up to sing a hymn or say the words in those small red books we can't see what's going on,' said Rachel.

'Most of the preachers use long words we don't understand,' said Deborah.

'Ask your parents then,' said Wez. 'My dad's got a brilliant vocabulary.'

'Well, mine's got a Volvo,' said Rachel, to several giggles.

'I do ask, but they don't know either,' continued Deborah. And they went on to mention the pews which, after ten minutes of sitting on them, gave you pins and needles in your bottom. The song slot was quite good. They did get a little fed up with singing about butterflies and 'Kings of the Jungle' – but realised that the younger ones liked them. But, worst of all, family services meant a week off from Discoverers.

'Well,' said Mr Orlando after considering their arguments, 'I think we should do something about this.'

'But what?' said Joel.

'Old Wobble would never change anything,' said Rachel immediately, not realising that she had called Reverend Wibble by his nickname until it was too late. Mr Orlando looked at her.

'Hmm, Old Wobble.'

'Sorry,' Rachel blurted, going red, 'it just slipped out.'

The others laughed. 'Reverend Wibble is all right,' said Mr Orlando, 'he tries to run the church so that as many people as possible enjoy being there.'

'But no-one ever listens to *us*,' said Jodi, and the others agreed with her, as they normally did.

'Have you ever said anything then? About the family services?' There was silence.

'Listen, you're just as important as anyone else in the

church. I'm sure if we could come up with an idea to do something ourselves towards the family services, Reverend Wobble, er Wibble would be thrilled.'

The Discoverers didn't look impressed. 'Oh, come on!' he continued, 'if you want to change something, you've got to *do* something, not just moan about it. Now, who's got an idea?' There was a pause whilst they thought. Then Stephen had an idea.

'We could write some poems.' The rest groaned.

'The time it takes you to write a poem it wouldn't be ready before Christmas,' said Wez, flicking a piece of paper at him.

'What about some pictures to decorate the back of the church?' said Rachel, to murmurs of interest.

'Or we could make a model or something,' said Jodi, always keen to use her hands.

'What about learning some songs to sing in the service?' added Adam – who liked singing almost as much as football.

Suddenly Joel leapt out of his chair and yelled, like he'd just sat on a drawing pin. Mr Orlando looked quite alarmed, but the others knew that this only meant that Joel had had an idea.

'A p-p-play,' he stammered, 'let's do a play.' The others then repeated their ideas at a louder volume, trying to outshout each other. Eventually, Mr Orlando slapped the table – and there was silence.

'Good,' said Mr Orlando. 'Good ideas – enough for a year's worth of services. I think we'd better start by offering something a little less . . . ambitious.' At this point he noticed Susan out of the corner of his eye. She had taken the general uproar as a chance to sit out and start thinking about her project. However, he didn't say anything, yet.

'I think there are some things which we can use, though. But what we need first is a theme or a title, to hold everything together. Susan, any ideas?' Susan looked up and straight into Mr Orlando's eyes, which were bright and twinkling – as if they were sharing a private joke with her, though she had no idea what.

'Er,' she jumped, and tried to cover with her arm the sheet of paper on which she'd got as far as writing the title of her project. An idea – help – what could she say? She looked down in desperation. All she could see was the title – she read it, and said simply, 'Caring for the World'.

'Brilliant!' said Mr Orlando very loudly, 'That's our topic – what shall we do?'

'What about all the things that are wrong with the world?' said Joel.

'OK,' said Mr Orlando. 'I need to write this down so we all remember. Can I borrow that paper, Susan?' And before she could protest, he'd whipped the sheet out from under her arm.

'There's a lot of plution,' said Rachel.

"P*ol*lution,' said Wez in the sort of voice which grown-ups often use when they want you to know they are being terribly patient.

'Yeah, my mum's in Friends of the Earth and she's always on about water being full of nasty gribley things which kill fish,' said Joel.

'And the air has got lots of lead in it,' added Deborah, remembering seeing signs for lead-free petrol.

'And seals die,' said Jodi.

'And birds get covered in oil,' said Adam.

Mr Orlando was writing all these things down, including the word 'gribley', which he loved.

'I read a book which said that the world is like a living planet,' said Stephen.

'Except it's dying,' said Susan. 'It's like the world is very, very sick . . . hang on, *that's it*!'

'What?' said the others.

'God's world is sick, humans have caused it, and we've got to care for it until it's better."

'Brrrilliant!' said Mr Orlando, catching Susan's excitement, 'you've done exactly what Jesus would have done,

Susan.'

'What?' said the others again.

'Well, if there was something he wanted to tell people about – he used a story or picture.'

'See, I said to use pictures!' said Rachel.

'Yes,' said Mr Orlando, 'but I don't quite mean painted ones. Susan has said "caring for the world, is like caring for a sick person".'

'But people live on the world – who lives in a person?' said Joel.

'We could pretend there are tiny people living in a human body,' said Susan.

'What do these tiny people do?' asked Mr Orlando.

Susan thought, then said, 'They work the body.'

'Great idea, Susan! Don't you agree, Discoverers?' They all nodded – except Wez, who looked miserable; he liked to have all the good ideas, especially about the world on which he knew tons of facts.

'Right, you can be the person in our story, Susan, and the rest of us will pretend to be the tiny people inside you – what shall they be called?'

'Bods,' said Susan.

'Bods it is. Right, help me move these tables. We'll have one for the Brain Bods.'

'I think I'll be the Brain Bods,' said Deborah.

'You'll *have* to think if you are,' joked Adam.

'Right you are,' said Mr Orlando. 'Now next to you are the Ear Bods – Jodi? Good – Eye Bods, Joel? – thank you. The Mouth Bods, now . . .' Everyone looked at Rachel.

'All right,' she said.

'Now then,' continued Mr Orlando, 'Stomach Bods.'

'Stephen's got the biggest one,' said Wez from the corner of the room. Stephen was an easy target. As he walked to the table that was to represent the stomach he wondered if he would ever get used to being laughed at.

'That just leaves the Leg and Arm Bods.'

Adam put up his hand and said, 'I'll be all four.'

Wez sat in the corner, wanting no part in this.

'Now, we're ready to begin. Once upon a time there was a girl called . . .' he stopped and looked at Susan.

'Anna,' said Susan.

'Called Anna. And Anna's body was worked by lots of tiny people called Bods. They were all very clever at their jobs and managed to make Anna's body work perfectly. Her brain could think.'

Deborah stuck her finger in her mouth and went cross-eyed. 'Duurrrr!'

The others laughed.

'Could think *properly*,' emphasised Mr Orlando, 'and swap messages with the other parts of the body. Her arms could move.'

'Move arms,' said Deborah. Adam pretended to move a big arm, and Susan waved her arms.

'Her eyes could see . . .' Joel used his hands like binoculars, and looked round the room, whilst Susan blinked.

'I can see a room, Brain Bod, with a boy sulking in the corner,' Joel said.

'The ears could hear.' Jodi put her hands behind her ears and swivelled her body like a radar.

'I can hear a pretty nifty story, Brain Bod.'

'And the mouth could talk and eat.' Rachel opened her mouth, and so did Susan.

'I'm hungry,' said Stephen the stomach, and he made a stomach rumbling noise.

'Good,' said Mr Orlando. 'Just at that moment, a sound entered Anna's ears.' And Mr Orlando said in a high voice, 'Anna, your dinner's on the table.'

Jodi was quick, as always. 'Ears to Brain, I've just heard that there's food on the table.'

Deborah responded: 'Brain to Legs, walk into the dining room.'

'Right you are,' said Adam.

'And swing the arms as well,' ordered Deborah, enjoying herself.

Anna started to walk into the 'dining room'.

'Watch out for that skateboard!' said Joel in the Eye department.

'Brain to Stomach, get ready for food,' said Deborah.

'Shloop! Shhllloooppp!' went Rachel. She stopped when the others looked at her questioningly, 'The mouth's watering!' she explained.

Mr Orlando continued the story. 'Soon Anna was eating fish and chips.' Rachel chewed imaginary food, then swallowed. 'Mouth to Stomach, it's on its way.' Stephen then made all sorts of gurgling noises.

'What's that?' said Deborah.

'Digestive noises,' replied Stephen.

Rachel put her hand up, grinning widely, and said, 'What's going to happen after the stomach?' They all thought, then laughed. 'Yes, well, let's leave that to your imaginations,' said Mr Orlando with a half laugh – half frown, then continued, 'So, Anna's body worked normally, and the Bods were happy in their jobs. Right, you can sit down whilst I finish the story.'

They did. 'For lurking in a corner of the body, almost unnoticed was . . . a Gribley. It lived in the appendix and fed on old bits of fat that were floating around. It was red and purple, with yellow eyes and a mouth that sagged open most of the time. But the worst thing was – it was selfish. And it wanted all the Bods to be selfish too.

'It went to the stomach and said, "Why bother to work so hard? Take life a bit easier – leave some of the food undigested and put your feet up." Stephen put his feet up with a sigh. After a while, Anna started to notice she was getting indigestion very badly. Then the Gribley went to the ears. "You're always listening to stuff you don't want to. Switch off and listen to your own kind of sounds." So the ears put on the loudest music it could think of. Anna started to get earache.

'Then the Gribley went to the eyes and said, "Work, work, work – don't worry about the rest of them – think of yourself. Relax, take it easy – have a soak in the tear container, here's some bubble bath". And Anna noticed that when she cried, her eyes stung like mad.

'The Gribley went round to all the different Bods and soon none of them wanted to work for Anna any more. They had all become content just looking after themselves. Of course, Anna became very ill. She couldn't walk properly, or use her arms – her mouth was dry, she had a headache, stomach-ache, backache, everything ache. Eventually she lay in bed, dying.'

The Discoverers looked sad.

'But,' continued Mr Orlando, enjoying the story, 'there was one Bod that the Gribley hadn't reached, the Heart Bod – I think Wez is the only one left.' Wez shrugged and tried to smile. 'It was responsible for Anna's feelings, and right now it was feeling very sad. It left the heart on "automatic" and went round the body – and wherever it went it saw Gribley-like Bods lazing around, doing nothing to help Anna.

The Heart Bod knew that they, the Bods, were the ones who kept Anna alive. There was not a moment to lose. It raced up to the brain, and persuaded it to remind Anna of a book she had on her book shelf. Anna pointed to it with a painful arm and her distraught mother, who was in the room, got it for her.

'Then, Wez the Heart Bod went all over the body, gathering up the other Bods and dragged them to the eye department. The Eye Bods had left the eyelids open, and Anna had just enough energy left to read the book.

'The book told of how God had wonderfully created humans and then made Bods to look after and enjoy them. It was their responsibility to care for the humans, and not just use them for their own pleasure. Because if Anna died, they would die too.

'The Bods were sad when they saw that they had neglected their duties. They all said sorry to God. Then they hurried back to their departments, and worked hard to get Anna's body well again. Anna was soon on the way to a full recovery. The end.'

The Discoverers clapped.

'Hooray for Wez,' said Jodi.

'But Mr Orlando, you said that we couldn't do any drama, so how will we do this story for the church?' said Joel, and the others nodded.

'You're quite right, Joel,' answered Mr Orlando. 'We can use the theme of "Caring for the World" though. Now the Bods was Susan's idea – I wonder if she has any use for it?' Susan now knew what that look in Mr Orlando's eyes had meant. He gave her back her sheet of paper, with most of the ideas they had just acted out on it. She had her assembly idea – and what an idea! The whole class could join in.

'Hang on, though,' said Wez, 'I think we ought to do something about Jesus or God – not something about nature and stuff.'

The others were silent.

'But Wez,' said Mr Orlando, 'who made the world? God. And who did he put in charge of it? Us. We've got more of a duty to care for it than anyone – its Creator is a friend of ours, after all.'

'Because if we forget the world, the world will die – and then we will too – just like Anna and the Bods,' said Stephen.

'Well done, Stephen – you see it's like the family services. If you want to change things, you've got to do something positive.'

Wez looked at the ground and said nothing – all his facts about mountains and rivers and planets firmly locked away inside his head.

'But what are we going to do next week, Mr Orlando?' said Stephen.

'Well, I've had an idea, but I'm afraid our time is up. Can anyone come early next week?' Seven hands shot up – Wez's followed reluctantly. 'Good,' said Mr Orlando. 'I'll explain it then.'

Stephen and the two trees

Sunday 25th November

Saturday morning had been a bad one for Stephen. He had been out shopping with his mum, carrying the bags as he always did. He had then spotted a local gang called the Recreation Street Wreckers hanging around the shopping centre. He shuffled towards them with his head down, cheeks red, sweat running down his face and glasses steaming up. As he approached, they called him several of their current favourite names; he hoped that his mum would think that they were shouting 'Incredible Bulk' at someone else. Then just as he was level with the gang, two of the plastic bags split at once – one containing a large unbreakable bottle of tomato sauce which, he discovered, wasn't unbreakable after all.

He was fed up with being the figure of fun, even in Discoverers. Why couldn't he be normal like everyone else? He couldn't play sport very well – unlike Adam. No girls really liked him – like they did Adam, and his handwriting was awful – unlike Adam's. It wasn't fair. That was when he had decided on the new haircut and clothes – and a new image.

Now he was outside the Discoverers' room, hearing the laughter and excitement going on inside. They were here early to prepare for the family service. They all lived close by so it was no problem. He took a deep breath and prepared to go in. As his hand touched the door handle he heard a voice behind him.

'What on earth has happened to you, Stephen? You look a real sight!' It was Wez. It would be. He was a bit late because he had had to say goodbye to his dad who was off to America on business for a few weeks . . . again. Stephen breathed deeply and tried hard to ignore the comment. This was part of his new plan. The old Stephen was no more; move aside for the new . . . Steve.

'It's Steve actually,' he said, and opened the door.

'. . . And what do you get if you cross a rooster with a poodle in a Chinese restaurant?' Rachel was saying, 'Cock-a-poodle-noodle-doodle-oo!' More laughter, which rapidly subsided when the group saw Stephen. He walked self-consciously to his place, trying to believe that there was nothing at all out of the ordinary.

Mr Orlando said, 'Ah, Wez, Stephen, here you are, now . . .'

'It's Steve, actually,' said Wez with a smirk, and sat down staring at Stephen with the rest of them.

Stephen's hair was usually straight, fairly long and parted to one side. Now it was short and gelled into spikes. It had looked OK yesterday when Colin the hairdresser had done it, but today when he had tried to do it himself, it didn't seem to have the same effect. His hair was quite fine, so rather than it all standing up evenly, it had gone into solid clumps of gel so his head looked a bit like the outside shell of a conker. His new trousers and shirt were supposed to make him look thinner. They were blue (Adam's favourite colour) and a whole size too small. He had discovered that if he breathed carefully, it wasn't too uncomfortable. He wasn't wearing a jumper. They continued to stare.

Eventually Wez said, 'He looks like a carrier bag that's just about ready to split.' The others usually ignored Wez's comments, but this time he happened to be right – and they all giggled. Stephen tried to laugh as well (another part of his new plan) but his tight trousers made it very difficult. He could feel his cheeks starting to warm up like an electric fire, so he dipped his head so the others wouldn't see, and sat down – very carefully.

'Now,' said Mr Orlando, 'I was just explaining that we're going to create a brilliant display for the back of the church. I thought if we were going to do something on "Caring for the World", we ought to go out and see a bit of it first. We'll pop into Colne Park to get some ideas. Now, come along, we haven't much time. You'd better decide whether you want to draw, paint, make, collect or write.' They all packed up paper and pencils; some took bags to collect bits and pieces.

It was only a short walk to the park – and as they walked with Mr Orlando, they discovered he could move at quite a pace. Stephen lagged behind, mainly because his trousers were so tight it was difficult to walk. When they arrived, each of them set about what they wanted to do.

Adam had decided to write a poem about the view from a tree, so he found the first one he could and proceeded to climb it. Jodi and Susan had decided to make something, so they were busily sketching ideas. Deborah had dragged Joel off (still a little upset at not being able to do a play) to collect some bits and pieces of nature. Rachel was walking slowly around on her own thinking about paintings, poems and stories (she wasn't sure which to do yet). Wez sat on an old log thinking. Stephen was usually happy just to sit and write about what he saw – but the new 'Steve' was different. He waited to see what Adam did, then 'decided' to climb a tree – a difficult tree, too.

After ten minutes or so, Mr Orlando, who had been doing some writing of his own, called everyone together. They started back to the church, talking excitedly about what they were going to do with the things and ideas they had collected. Mr Orlando said nothing, but just thought.

He remembered the telephone conversation that he'd had last Tuesday. Reverend Wibble had explained that '*he* had nothing against the Discoverers doing *something* at the back of church. However, there were *certain* people who wouldn't take kindly to having displays and goodness-knows-what *cluttering up* the place, and he was sure that Mr Orlando would under*stand*.' Mr Orlando did understand grown ups, after all he'd been one himself for many years.

Suddenly he realised that he had only seven Discoverers. Stephen was missing, and they were nearly back at the church. He told the others to go on and walked back to Colne Park. It wasn't long before he saw Stephen's blue trousers sticking out from below a branch in a tree. He walked to the tree and looked up. Stephen was sitting there, his face and clothes blotched in dirt and moss. His eyes were fixed on a distant point.

'The others have gone back,' said Mr Orlando.

'Oh?' was the reply. Stephen didn't look down.

'There isn't much time to prepare.' Silence. 'Do you want a hand down?'

'No, thanks,' said Stephen, 'I just want to look at the view – then I may come back, or I may not.' He had decided that it was cool to be uninterested in things, even if he was terrifically interested really.

Mr Orlando continued, 'Stephen . . .'

'Steve!'

'Stephen!' Stephen looked down. 'God made you as Stephen. Steve is someone you've made yourself.'

'What does God know?' said Stephen.

'Well, quite a lot actually.'

'Then why didn't he make me normal, like everyone else?'

'Stephen, what is normal? Everyone's different – and God loves us equally – for who we are. I know it's a pity that not all people see that too . . .'

'But I want to be cool.'

'Well why don't you put on a white box and pretend to be a fridge then?' said Mr Orlando with a smile. Stephen nearly smiled too, but didn't, or rather couldn't. 'Stephen,' he continued, 'God's happiest when you are yourself. I know it's not always easy, but in the end it's the best you can be.'

'I'm useless – I'm just a problem.'

'The only problem you are to me is that this whole display thing is relying on you. I need you to write a poem, not sit in a tree like a koala on strike.' Stephen looked interested. 'Come on.' And Mr Orlando started to walk away.

A call from Stephen stopped him. 'I can't.'

Mr Orlando looked up and Stephen slowly took his hands away from where he'd been holding his trousers together. The button had completely come off because of the pressure of his stomach. Mr Orlando helped Stephen to jump down, and then took off his own belt and gave it to him. It fitted, just – though only on the narrowest setting as Mr Orlando wasn't exactly thin.

'That should take care of it,' he said.

'But won't your trousers fall down?' asked Stephen.

'I always wear braces as well as a belt. A silly little habit of mine. Now do come on,' and they hurried off together.

When they got back, the others had already started work. Susan and Jodi had begun cutting out a huge tree from cardboard, and Rachel was busily mixing up some green and brown paints. The rest were arranging bits of bark and cones and suchlike into a sort of, well, arrangement to be at the bottom of the tree. All, that is, except Wez; he was just poking about with a fir cone, much too pleased about Stephen's problems to do anything. It was good to have someone in trouble.

'Ah,' said Mr Orlando when he entered the room and saw the activity.

'We thought we'd better start,' said Jodi, whose decision it had been. 'did you want to do something else?'

'No, no,' assured Mr Orlando, though he had intended something different.

'But you told me that poems were important, not painting and stuff!' said Stephen. Mr Orlando thought hard.

'And so they are, Stephen.' He looked at the tree.

'Rrrright!' he said at last. 'Susan and Jodi, start the painting – everyone else grab some paper – we're going to create poetry or rather, a poet-tree! We'll all write a poem about caring for God's world – remember the topics we talked about last week? Then we'll stick them on the branches like leaves. What a brilliant idea for a display – well done, everyone!'

Stephen was happier, but Wez wasn't. Not only had Stephen got the chance to make up for this morning, but they had to make up poems, at which he was useless. Suddenly, he had an idea. Stephen was collecting some paper. Now was his chance to act.

Stephen settled down to write a poem – he had a great idea. He went to pick up his pen – it was gone. He looked all over the place, but it was nowhere to be seen. He was just about to go and ask Deborah if he could borrow one, when Wez leaned over to him.

'Lost your pen, Steve?' Stephen, who hadn't forgotten the carrier bag joke, just nodded. 'Here, use this one.' He held out a pen. Stephen thought about it, and after deciding that it was a kind gesture, accepted it with a simple 'Thanks'. He took off the lid – it was a beautiful fountain pen, with a shiny gold nib. Great! He'd be able to write more neatly as well.

He set to work and soon realised it was one of the best poems he'd ever written. The more he wrote, the more excited he got. Eventually, on the last line the inevitable happened – there was a 'thd!'. Stephen looked at the inkblot on his work – then at the twisted metal that used to be the nib. He could feel the beginnings of a sweat on his forehead, his glasses began to steam up. Still, Wez would understand – he was always on about how many things his dad gave him – and he could offer to buy him a new pen. He leaned over, but Wez was already looking at him. 'Sorry,' said Stephen with difficulty, 'I, er, seemed to have . . .' 'It's not me you have to say sorry to,' replied Wez.

'It's Mr Orlando's pen – didn't I tell you?'

Stephen was horrified. For a whole ten seconds he just stared at the broken pen. When he spoke, it was only a feeble, 'What shall I do?'

This was what Wez had been waiting for. 'Don't worry *Steve*, I won't tell anyone. I'll keep hold of the pen, and he'll think he's lost it.'

Stephen wasn't sure this was right, but he didn't have the energy to think properly, so he just said, 'Thanks.'

'However,' Wez went on, 'there's one small thing I want in return,' and he took Stephen's poem. 'Ta. Don't worry – no-one will know when I've written it out in my own handwriting. Oh look, here's your pen, it must have fallen into my pocket by mistake.' And he gave Stephen his pen back.

Mr Orlando slapped his table. 'Rrright, ten minutes left – let's start getting the poems together – wow! Fantastic tree, you two.' And it was. The Discoverers started sticking their poems on to the tree – Stephen sat in the corner scribbling madly. Luckily he had had another idea, but there was only time to jot it down in short lines.

Soon the tree was covered in poems. Mr Orlando had written a sign saying: 'Discoverers' Re-cycled Poet-tree', which he put on the top, whilst reminding the group that the re-cycled paper they had been using saved too many trees from having to be cut down. They were just about to leave for the service when Stephen rushed up with his new poem.

'Oh, bad luck, there's no room, Steve,' sneered Wez.

'Hold on,' said Mr Orlando, 'we've forgotten the most important place.' And he took Stephen's poem. Because it was composed of short lines and was rather long and narrow, he put it on the trunk. 'There – the poem to support all the others.'

They took the display to the church and arranged it at the back with just minutes to spare.

After the service, people spent a long time looking at the large tree with its crop of poems, and its forest floor display. Adam came up to Stephen, and, looking a bit shifty, said, 'Do you like my poem?'

Stephen realised he hadn't even read it – so he did now. 'It's very good, Adam.'

'Thanks, only I thought – well, I er, really like your poems, and I tried to write like you, a bit – hope you don't mind.' Stephen was speechless.

Adam continued, 'I see Wez has too – it's just like one you would have written. Still, it's not as good as yours, Steve.'

'Stephen,' said Stephen.

The people in St Margaret's were thrilled at the display – except for a small group who disliked new ideas. Mr Orlando saw one of them talking at length to Reverend Wibble before coming over to where the Discoverers were standing.

'Come along, Wesley, your lunch will spoil.' Wez left with his mum as Reverend Wibble arrived.

'Well done, Mr Orlando, *splendid* display – how clever of you to know that Nick would be speaking about our responsibility for the *world* today – he couldn't have wished for a better visual *aid*. I must chat to you about the Christmas family *service* next month.'

He started to walk away with Mr Orlando, who before he went, pressed a piece of paper into Stephen's hand and said, 'Here's my poem, for what it's worth.'

Here is a copy of the poem that Mr Orlando gave to Stephen. After it are the poems that were on the poet-tree.

A poem for Stephen by Orlando

Can you imagine one fine day,
Waking from your slumbers,
To find that all the clouds are painted
Greener than cucumbers?

Or opening your bedroom curtains
To admire the view,
And seeing all the trees are now
A luminousy blue?

Then hearing there are elephants
Being taught to ride on bikes,
And conger eels encouraged to
Go jogging wearing spikes?

Of course, you say, it's the most stupid
Thing I've ever heard.
A tree's a tree, a bee's a bee
And every bird's a bird.
It's wrong to change the way things are,
As well as quite absurd.

But when we say 'I don't like me'
We tamper with creation,
And try to change what God has made
To pale impersonations.

God has made us all unique,
It's absolutely true.
There's no-one in the world the same.
God's chuffed that you are *you*.

(And so am I, Stephen.)

The tree by Wez

I'm standing in a field
My arms are lifted to my Creator,
They say 'Praise my God'
– like a psalm.

My trunk gives homes to squirrels,
My leaves give food to grubs and bugs,
My twigs will be for birds
To build their nests in my branches.

My fruit is for animals in snow
Who use my shade in sun.
My leaves when fallen enrich the soil
That is held together by my roots.

I wake in spring
And sleep in winter
Then wake in spring.

Now my arms are lifted to my Creator,
And say 'Help me, help me.'

A man is coming
I would offer him everything
In life.
But he wants to take everything
In death.
His saw buzzes and I die.
My end is a crash and a crush –
I fall on my friends.

In a day my carcase will be split.
In two days I will be in your hands
As a book or a mag.
On the third day
I will be in my tomb.

I cannot rise again
From your wastepaper bin.

One Body by Rachel

Pretend the world is like a body.
Alive and well.
And we are the peopel who live in it.
(I am a mouth).
But the Gribblees will make me lazie.
And not take care of the body.

The world will die,
And so will I.

The Gifts by Adam

Look around the park
What do I see?
A lovely nature garden
A gift to you and me.

Look around the park
What do I see?
Empty cans and plastic bottles
Gifts *from* you and me.

Oi, you lot! by Deborah

Hands off our world, you lot.
Stop killing our seals, you lot.
Leave our trees alone, you lot
Quit robbing our seas of whales, you lot.
Pack in polluting our rivers, you lot.

You know it's God's world.
You don't know how to look after it.

The Story Of The World by Joel

Tell me a story, world, about your birth.
'I came to be with a swoosh and a swirl,
I flew into place at God's command.'

Tell me a story, world, about your life.
'I was home for creation, all things alive,
Everything loved me, except for mankind.'

Tell me a story, world, about your death.
'There wasn't a sound nor a nuclear blast,
I just fizzled out as I ran out of breath.'

Care For God's World by Stephen

Wind
caresses
grass.
Trees
clap
hands.
Flowers
feed
bees.
Sea
strokes
shores.
Hills
protect
valleys.
Plants
house
insects.
Jungles
shade
animals.
God made the
world to care for
his creation. So let
us all CARE FOR GOD'S WORLD.

Jodi has a birthday to remember

Sunday 2nd December

Adam picked up Jodi's present and left his house. He had been saving up for quite a while, and had bought her the Michael Jackson T-shirt she wanted. He was late as he had stayed in bed a bit too long thinking of yesterday's football match: the final of the under-11 District Cup. Adam had been playing for his new team Hanworth Rovers, who had won 2-1.

He decided to take a short cut through Recreation Street. This was not a route he would normally take nowadays as Roger Frewin lived there. Roger Frewin had heard all about Adam's new team, the Rovers, and was not pleased. News was out that he wanted to 'see' Adam.

Roger was about the same size as Adam. His hair was never combed and looked like a rook's nest. His front teeth stuck out, earning him the nickname of 'Roger Rabbit'. Though since he had joined the 'Wreckers', Roger's brother's gang, no-one had dared call him that.

When the gang weren't practising their graffiti at the shopping centre, they just hung about outside Roger's house, kicking bottles or pushing each other through people's hedges. Adam reckoned that Sunday morning would be safe enough – it was worth the risk.

He turned off the main road into Recreation Street. He walked briskly, and passed by a man who was taking his dog for a walk in the opposite direction. The man's Alsatian strained at the lead for a sniff of Adam's leg – at least Adam hoped it was for a sniff.

'It's all right, son, he won't hurt you – he's friendly, aren't you, Sabre?' Not convinced, Adam gave the dog a wide berth. He walked on, and eventually rounded the bend bringing Roger's house into view. His heart leapt – with relief – the house was quiet and still.

Just to be safe he crossed over to the other side of the road. As he approached the house, he looked at its grey net curtains, broken front gate and scruffy front door which was now opening, and . . . It was too late – Roger and three other boys had seen him. 'Oh look, lads, it's Adam of the Rovers,' said Roger as they hurried over the road. They blocked the path so he couldn't continue on his journey.

'Smart ain't he, lovely clothes,' said one of the gang, who was as big as an American footballer, even without the padding.

'What's this?' Roger reached for the birthday present. Adam moved it out of his reach.

'It's a present, if you must know,' said Adam, trying not to sound as frightened as he was. 'Look, let me go. I'm late for . . .'

'For what?' said Roger.

'Well, it's a sort of birthday party,' Adam said, and tried to walk – the gang closed ranks.

'It's my friend's birthday as well,' Roger indicated the enormous one. 'Where's *his* present?'

'I don't know,' said Adam.

'Well, we'll have to have this one then.' And one of the boys standing behind him snatched the present from his grasp and read the label, slowly.

'To – Jo – die. Jo-die? what sort of a stupid name is that?' Roger took the present.

'Jodi, you thick nurk, and I know what kind of name it is – it's a Rasta name.' Rasta was what Roger called all black people. 'I've seen you two up the town in Wimpy's. 'Fact I've been meaning to talk to you for some time. You see, we don't like kids who go around with *them* – so if you want this,' he held up the present, 'you'll have to fight for it.'

Adam was silent. Then he said, 'I don't believe in fighting.' The others laughed, then the one behind him shoved Adam forward so he crashed into Roger, who started hitting him.

Have you ever noticed that real fights aren't like the neat and tidy ones you see in films:

Sock! Thump! Argh! Pow!

Real fights are ugly, with windmill arms getting in as many punches as possible, no matter where they land.

Yarghthumpugheekyaheechurrggh!

Adam hit Roger a couple of times, but he knew it was useless – so he lifted up his hands to protect his head. After a while, he fell to the ground and felt a sharp pain in his stomach where one of the bigger ones kicked him. Then they left him, and he heard their laughter disappearing down the road along with the sound of ripping paper. He tried to move, but the pain in his stomach was too great.

He was still there when Jodi found him.

Meanwhile, back at Discoverers, Rachel was in full flow. '. . . then my mum said to me "All you do is sit and watch that awful Australian programme and never help me lay the table." So I said to her that I was obeying the Bible – then she said "How?" and I said "Cause it says love your neighbours, doesn't it"?' and everyone laughed.

'OK cobbers, get to your places,' said Mr Orlando in a very good Australian accent. When they had settled down he continued, 'Now I think Jodi must be busy with her family's presents – though I don't know where Adam has got to? Anyway, I was talking about neighbours, and Rachel is right, it does say love your neighbour. What does it mean?'

Eventually Joel said, 'Be kind to people.'

'Yes, that's the nub of it. But which people?'

'People next door,' said Deborah.

'Ye-e-es,' said Mr Orlando, waiting for more answers.

'People in your street?' tried Susan.

'Your family and friends,' said Rachel.

In another part of the circle, Wez was taunting Stephen with Mr Orlando's broken pen, which he still had.

'People you don't like,' said Stephen.

'Now that's more like it, Stephen. Can anyone think of a story Jesus told about someone being kind to someone they didn't like?'

They thought for a bit, before Joel said, 'The good Samaritan.'

'Rrrright! It gave the listeners such a surprise – because Jesus was saying that *everyone* is our neighbour.'

'But I can't love people I don't like,' grunted Deborah.

'Nor me,' added Wez, 'I'd rather use something from my "Practical Jokes" book to get my own back.' And he secretly put Mr Orlando's pen in Stephen's pencil case, meaning to 'find' it later when everyone was watching.

'Well, Jesus meant that we should treat everyone the same way – the way we would like them to treat us. I know, we'll all draw a cartoon strip that is like a modern version of the Good Samaritan. Jesus' audience thought the Samaritans were the least likely to help anyone. Who would be the least likely to help anyone these days?'

Just then, Jodi came in and slumped down in a seat.

'Ah Jodi,' said Mr Orlando, 'we were just talking about the Good Samaritan – and how although it's hard, Jesus wants us to be kind to everyone, even those we think are horrible.' He noticed her looking sad. 'Oh, of course,' he went on, 'how stupid of me – your birthday presents! Sorry – if you don't mind, you can have them later, when Adam gets here —'

'He won't be here,' said Jodi, and slowly told them all about the events of that morning. She finished up, 'and then I took him home and his dad said he'd get Frewin.'

'Poor Adam,' said Orlando at length, 'though I'm not sure that his father's solution would be right.'

'Why not? Adam wasn't doing anything wrong. I'd smash his head in,' came a voice.

'But, Deborah,' said Mr Orlando, 'it wouldn't end there. You hit them, they hit you again, and before you know where you are, someone really gets hurt. Violence only ever leads to more violence.'

'But I'm not going to be a wimp, and stand by and let my friends be picked on,' she argued.

Mr Orlando understood why she said this. 'I'm not saying it's easy, Deborah. You'll discover that it's actually braver *not* to fight, to stand up for what you know is right. If you live by being tough, then that's how people treat you . . . I know. Now Jodi, you –'

'I haven't finished yet,' she said quietly. 'On my way here, I went down Recreation Street again. I was really cross, fuming cross. As I got to the middle of the road, I saw Roger Rabbit.' The others didn't giggle, although Rachel thought one. 'He was heading towards me on his bike. As he got near me he slowed down and said something like "I sorted out your lover boy, Rasta". As he came level I was really angry, so I picked up a stick and threw it at him.'

'Did you hit him?' said Deborah hopefully.

'No, but I hit the bike. The stick went through the spokes of the front wheel and made the bike stop suddenly.' Her voice started to give way to emotion. 'He flew over the top and hit the road. There was a huge crack and . . .I think his arm broke and he started howling.'

A shocked gasp from the others.

'What did you do?' said Joel.

'Well, there was this woman who was walking past, and . . .'

'Did she help?' interrupted Susan.

'No, she just said "stupid kids" and carried on.'

'Then what?' Even Wez was intrigued.

'It's just like the Good Samaritan,' said Rachel. 'Did you help him like in the story?'

'Well,' Jodi said again, 'I . . . ran away,'

'You ran away?' they all said in various ways.

'Yes, I just ran all the way here and left him and . . . now I, oh . . .' And she dissolved into tears. The rest comforted her with words which ranged from Rachel's 'Never mind, it'll be OK', to Deborah's, 'We'll sort them out all right'.

After a while, the door opened, and Adam walked in, rather gingerly. Everyone welcomed him warmly.

'Didn't expect to see you today,' said Mr Orlando.

'I feel a bit better now – I couldn't stand being in the house with my dad shouting about getting them back – and I wanted to apologise to Jodi for not having her present.'

'Don't worry about that, stupid,' said Jodi. The others then filled him in on what had happened to Roger Frewin.

When they had finished he said, 'Oh, that would explain the ambulance.'

'What ambulance?' said Jodi.

'As I was coming down the main road, I saw one pulling out of Recreation Street – that must have been Roger on his way to hospital. And . . .' Adam stopped short.

'And what?' said Deborah.

'Well, I saw two of the gang. They stopped me, and asked if I knew who'd done it. When I said I didn't, they said they were going to get whoever had.' The room fell silent.

'There you are,' said Deborah at long last, 'we've got to defend ourselves!'

'I don't know what came over me,' said Jodi. 'I'm quite used to people treating me differently because I'm black. My family have been turned out of shops, and my mum's had horrible things shouted at her from cars. Whenever anyone picks on us, she always tells us to say, 'You're only jealous you're not black'. But it was when Adam got hurt, just because of me, I . . . I . . .'

There was a slight pause before Mr Orlando said, 'I don't know, you lot – you get yourselves into some right old pickles. Well, fortunately we've got a friend who's been through it all. Come on, let's pray. Dear Lord Jesus – well, here we are again, asking for your help. Thank you that you made us all, and that you have asked us to care for your creation by looking after one another. Please help Adam to get better soon – and Roger, of course. And help Jodi to know what to do. Amen.'

They all repeated the 'Amen'. It was always fantastic how, when Mr Orlando prayed, you knew that Jesus was right there with you. Mr Orlando looked at his watch.

'Oh dear,' he said, 'we've run out of time again.'

'I'm going to go round to Roger's house,' said Jodi quietly.

'To say "serves you right"?' said Rachel.

'To bash him? I'll come,' said Deborah.

'I don't know why yet, but I will when I get there.'

'I'm sure you will, Jodi,' said Mr Orlando, 'I'll pray for you. Sorry we've run out of time. First thing next week, we'll have your present openings, OK? Go on then, push off!' And they did – Wez forgetting all about the pen in Stephen's pencil case, and Stephen forgetting all about his pencil case, which he left on the table.

Later that afternoon, Jodi was walking once more down Recreation Street. On her left was Adam, and on her right was Deborah, who had come along 'to protect Jodi if things got nasty'. They went up the path and knocked on the door. Inside, a dog started barking loudly. They heard a voice.

'Shut up, Sabre – Sabre! Shut up!' Eventually the door opened and Mr Frewin stood there, holding back the Alsatian by his studded collar.

'Sabre, get down – yeah, what is it?' he said to them.

'Is Roger in?' asked Jodi, her heart beating so loudly she thought Mr Frewin must be able to hear it.

'Yeah, he's in the lounge.' He opened the door and let them in – then, closing the front door, he pushed the door of the lounge open with his foot. They walked in and stood, kneecaps quivering.

Roger was sitting on a leather sofa, one arm in a sling, the other holding a cigarette. Sitting around him were his brother and two others. They all looked up. Roger's face went through various expressions – sneer, dislike, wonder, another sneer, and then settled on a curious sort of horror.

'Oh look, Rovers and Rasta. What d'you want?' he said, and they noticed that one of his front teeth was broken as well as his arm.

'I, er . . . um,' said Jodi.

'We heard you were looking for the people that got your arm broke,' said Deborah. She spoke their language.

'Yeah,' one said.

'And when we get 'em we're going to mash 'em into tiny bits,' said the second.

'Then go and stuff 'em down the drains,' said Roger's brother – they all laughed. 'That Station Road gang have asked for it this time. No-one breaks a Wrecker's arm and lives, eh Rog?'

Roger looked at the ground and said a feeble, 'No.'

Jodi opened her mouth to speak, but Deborah was in first. 'What you on about, Station Road gang? My mate here did it.' The three lads looked slowly from Deborah to Adam.

'You?' they said.

'Er, well . . .' stuttered Adam.

'No, it was me.' The gang's heads turned to Jodi.

'YOU?' they said again, in disbelief.

'Yes – and I wanted to say I was, er kind of, er sorry' ' The end of her apology was lost in the barrage of questions that Roger was undergoing.

'You said it was the Station Road Gang!'

'You said there were five of them!'

'Lucky to escape with your life, were you?'

'You should have seen what I did to them, was it?'

'Come on, lads, I'm going,' said Roger's brother. 'I knew it was stupid to let my kid brother join a man's gang. You're out, son, O – W – T, out!' And they pushed past the Discoverers and left.

Roger was left, with a broken arm, and no friends.

'If you live by being tough, then that's how people treat you,' said Deborah, quietly.

'What?' said Adam.

'Nothing,' she replied, and glared at Roger. Jodi was trying to think what to do. She could easily get her own back now – but then . . .

She tried not to think about the Good Samaritan, but couldn't help it. Treat everybody the same – she guessed that meant also not kicking someone when they were down. It was so hard though. 'Look,' she said, not really sure what she was going to say, 'er, I'm sorry about your arm, and your gang.'

'Cheers,' sneered Roger, ungratefully.

'If you want, you can come to our sort of . . . gang next Sunday if you like.' (She couldn't believe she was saying this.)

'What gang?' Roger was almost interested.

'It's, er, called the Discoverers gang.'

'Might.'

'Oh, great, well, er, we'll see you then,' said Jodi.

Deborah, wanting to leave him with a good last line, said 'Count your lucky stars, kid,' mixing up 'count your blessings' and 'thank your lucky stars'.

Adam went, followed by Deborah. As Jodi left she turned back. 'Oh, Roger,' she said, 'where did you get that brill T-shirt? I love Michael Jackson.'

Rachel and the prodigal gerbil

Sunday 9th December

Someone incredibly amazing was to visit St Margaret's and outside the church, the crowd was waiting anxiously. The police had erected crash barriers to stop people spilling on to the road, as they might get their feet on the red carpet. There was a special section for the press which had two TV camera teams, countless reporters, and photographers with lenses like telescopes. The Discoverers were waiting by the door to welcome this most Very Important Person to their church. One of them was going to present a bouquet and make a short welcome speech. Rachel clutched the flowers, stood up straight and felt an electric current of excitement as she saw the Queen's car coming along the main road, which was lined with thousands of tiptoed wavers.

The big, black limousine pulled up, the little flag on the top of the car flapping busily in the breeze. An official man at the roadside opened the car door and out stepped the Queen to a huge Union Jack cheer. She was wearing a bright green dress with a matching hat. Rachel thought she looked just like she does on coins. The Queen took a few steps forward, then stopped and smiled at the Discoverers.

Rachel stepped forward with all the confidence she possessed and did a neat curtsy. Then she offered the flowers to the Queen. 'Your majesty,' she began in a nice clear voice, the cameras clicking and whirring, 'these are for you, to welcome you to St Margaret's church. We do hope that you will enjoy your visit to us.' Everyone clapped, and Rachel backed away from the Queen, as she'd been told to do at the special practice. This was the proudest moment of her life.

But just as she began to feel relief soak into her every muscle, the Queen said, 'You're called Rachel, aren't you?' Rachel was taken aback.

'Yes ma'am,' she said, pronouncing it correctly, 'marm'.

'And are these your friends?' the Queen went on.

'Yes ma'am, we're called the Discoverers.'

'Oh, and what would one discover in Discoverers?'

'Lots of things – our leader Mr Orlando is so clever. That's him there.' The Queen looked towards Mr Orlando and smiled. Mr Orlando, bowing low, said:

'Rachel? Rachel, are you with us? Hello, is anyone at home?' Rachel woke from her daydream and saw Mr Orlando looking at her. His face looked as though he was waiting for an answer to some question she hadn't heard.

'Pardon?' she said, feebly.

'I said we're off for a quick game of indoor hockey. The others are all ready – hurry up, see you in the hall.' Mr Orlando led the others through the door for this week's game. Rachel, the memory of her daydream fast fading, wasn't all that keen on indoor hockey. Susan was much better than her, and everyone was always saying how good she was at scoring goals. It was hard having an older sister who seemed to be so good at so many things. She had always been called 'the slow one' at home. The only thing she could do was tell jokes and make people laugh. Why couldn't life be like her day-dream?

She pulled on her trainers, a pair of Susan's old ones which were still a bit big. They had frayed laces, and a hole appearing in the left toe. It was then that she saw it, sitting in the open pencil case.

The pen was mainly brown, with beautiful swirls and spirals of other colours including gold, a bit like seeing petrol in a puddle. It was so pretty : she just *had* to touch it. How smooth it was, just like marble. Rachel had never taken anything in her life until that moment. She was amazed at how easy it was – the sky didn't fall in, and God didn't shout 'Stop it!' from heaven. With the pen in her pocket she went out to play hockey. As she got there she felt that everyone must surely know – her pocket felt transparent. But the first thing she heard was Susan saying, 'Come on, Rach, you're in goal – just for a bit.' Rachel knew this meant the whole game.

Afterwards they filed back into their room, puffing and panting, the winning team congratulating themselves on their skill – especially Susan's – the unfortunate losers promising Rachel that she wouldn't be asked to go in goal again, like they always did.

'I'm so glad my dad has taken me to so many ice hockey games, it really paid off,' said Wez, who had managed to score – well, a shot of Susan's had hit him on the way into the goal.

But Rachel couldn't even remember the game – she had been miles away. She really regretted taking the pen. She thought about trying to slip it back into the pencil case, but it had been zipped up. She sat there feeling guiltier than she had ever felt in her whole life.

'Rrrright,' said Mr Orlando, his eyes as bright as always. 'Good news. Reverend Wobble, er Wibble, thought the poet-tree we all did for the family service two weeks ago was great. And he wants us to do something for the special Christmas service in two weeks time!'

The Discoverers cheered heartily – except for Wez, whose mother had not liked what they'd done then, and Rachel who had not liked what she'd done just now. Wez gave the appearance of being pleased, and to show it he said, 'Must have been my brilliant poem, eh Steve?' Stephen just stared ahead, and worried more about Mr Orlando's broken pen, which he still hadn't owned up to.

'What shall we do?' said Jodi.

'We'll discuss it in a minute. Let's pray first. Now

let's see, who can say a prayer for us . . .' He looked around the room meeting every eye but Rachel's, who was hoping against all hope that she wouldn't be picked. How could she possibly speak to God? He had seen her terrible crime – so bad that she doubted if she could ever be forgiven. Mr Orlando noticed Rachel's mood and as a result, changed his plans '. . . after the story.'

'Story?' said Joel.

'Yes, we haven't had one for a while. Rachel, choose an animal.'

Rachel was caught off guard, and simply said, 'Gerbil,' as she had two.

'Good, now an object.'

'A pen – NO! er, a crown.'

'And a place.'

'Bathroom,' she said, wishing she was in one – anywhere but here.

'Right, this is the story of King Gerbil the second,' announced Mr Orlando. 'There was once a King called King Gerbil II, ruler over where?'

'West Gerbilly,' said Joel.

'Right. King Gerbil II was a funny old stick – his court room was in a bathroom. This was because the rest of the palace was made of chewed up paper and mud, so he was always getting very dirty and needing a wash. His throne was the . . .'

'Toilet!' they all said at once.

'Which had a nice green fluffy seat cover to make it comfortable. King Gerbil II loved crowns so much that he had spent all his money on having the best one ever made for him. Now the King had two daughters, called?'

'Enid,' said Adam, who had seen the name on one of his brother's books.

'And Rachel,' said Susan, who had also sensed something was wrong with her sister, and wanted her to be included.

'One day, Princess Rachel came to her father and said, "Daddy, when will I receive my fortune?"

"When I die," said the king.

"Well, I want it now!" said Princess Rachel, stamping her foot. "I wish you were dead so I could be rich." This is a horrible thing to say to anyone, let alone your father. King Gerbil II was very sad, but not stupid. He wasn't going off to Gerbilheaven yet, not for anyone – he had a ticket for the Royal Hockey Final next week between the Hemel Hempstead Hamsters and the New Guinea Guinea Pigs. He thought for a minute, then slowly, he took off his crown.

"Royal crownsmith," he said, "take my crown and saw it in half."

'A murmur ran round the court room – and got very puffed. "With one half, make me a new crown. With the other, cash in the gold and the diamonds and give the money to the Princess."

"And make sure it's the biggest half," said Princess Rachel.

'When Princess Rachel got her money she left the Palace without so much as a goodbye. She went to buy a train ticket, but then remembered she had loadsamoney, and bought a ticket for Concorde. She travelled in the best seat, and had lots of glasses of a special fizzy drink which made her whiskers twitch.

'When she arrived in America, she immediately got to work spending her fortune. "What's the point of having money if you don't spend it?" she thought. Rachel bought a car which was so long that it would take you five minutes to roller skate round it. She hired a chauffeur to drive her everywhere, especially to the Amazing Amusement Casino R.G.O. (Rich Gerbils Only) where there were lots of favourites, which were . . .'

'Fighter Pilot,' said Deborah, the group expert on video games.

'Good one – you had to shoot down enemy aeroplanes before they got you. When you were blown up, the whole machine shook with the explosion, and smoke came out of the sides.'

'Grath, Overlord of the Universe,' added Adam, who had seen it in the local chip shop.

'Right,' said Orlando, 'with this one you had to save the universe from attack by the Vikogremlins, but Princess Rachel never did.

'Now it's fun to play these games occasionally, but Princess Rachel went there every day and every night. She played them all the time. She perfected the art of driving "Revenge Gerbil Jet-bikes of Galaxy 4" one-handed whilst she ate her rump steak burgers and caviare with the other. She became very popular in the casino with the owners and the other players. She made, or rather bought, lots of friends because she gave them money to play the machines.

'After a few weeks of this spending, Princess Rachel went from rich to quite rich, then to well off, then to comfortable, ordinary, quite poor, very poor, completely broke and finally to owing a lot of money. She asked her friends for a loan, but they only laughed. Princess Rachel was about as popular as a surprise maths test on a Friday afternoon.

"Things can't get any worse," she sobbed.

"Yes they could," said the casino owner, "here's your food bill – $10,987." She said she couldn't pay, and was thrown out by four enormous Guinea Pigs dressed in posh suits.

'On the street she started to cry. She'd had to sell her car to pay for her high living, so she started walking around wondering where her next meal was coming from. After a week without anything to eat, her old chauffeur came by. He told her that his new boss Lord Tom, the richest cat in New York, might have a job for her if she came straight away. She went to climb in the back of the car, but she was in such an awful pongy state she had to go in the boot.

'Still, at least she had a job to look forward to. But it turned out to be fattening up Lord Tom's mice ready for eating. She fed them the best nuts and cheese, but wasn't allowed to eat any herself. In the yard where the mice lived was the oldest, dirtiest shed you could imagine. It was really smelly, and had massive spiders lurking in every corner. This was where Princess Rachel had to sleep.

'After a week, she could stand it no more. "Man, I am in Grubsville," she said, having picked up some American phrases. "Even King Daddy's servants live better than this. If Daddy would have me back I could offer to be the Royal paper chewer, the worst job in the palace – anything would be better than this. It's worth a try – I suppose."

'Leaving the house, she found her way to the port and begged to be let on board a ship to West Gerbilly if she scrubbed out the galley every day. Soon she was back in her home country, and started the eighty-one mile walk home.

'As she got nearer, she started to dread seeing her father again. She knew he had a temper and would probably shout at her – even have her whipped with the "mouse o' nine tails". Then as she approached the palace itself, her heart sank. Her father (with the Royal guard) was running towards her. She thought he had a horrible grin on his face and tears of hatred in his eyes. She cowered by the side of the road and waited for the first blow.

'But instead of pain, she felt her father's arms around her, and her fur getting wet from his tears – not of anger, but of joy. He took her into the palace and gave her the biggest welcome home party the gerbil world has ever seen. The end.'

The group buzzed as they talked about what the party would have been like. Eventually Mr Orlando said: 'Surprise, surprise!'

'Not really,' said Jodi, 'it's the story of the Prodigal Son isn't it, from the Bible? I knew what was going to happen.'

'Rrrright, Jodi – but just imagine being Princess

Rachel – feeling you'd done something so awful you could never be forgiven, and then – forgiveness! and that's how God forgives us.'

Rachel *did* feel like Princess Rachel, but surely God couldn't forgive her for . . . she hardly dared think the word, stealing? 'And what's more, he doesn't just say, "Oh all right, I'll forgive you, you measly worm." He says . . . "*Yippeeeee*! Welcome back. Up here in heaven we're so chuffed that we're going to have a party even bigger than King Gerbil II's. If,' and now Mr Orlando looked as serious as he had been jolly a split second before, 'if you are sorry, and you're really, honestly, truthfully sorry".'

He smiled again, and said, 'Hands up if the Queen knows your name.' No–one moved. Rachel started, then remembered that it was only in her daydream. 'Right, but you'd think it was wonderful if she did, wouldn't you?' They all nodded, except Rachel, who was near to tears, but held them back. 'Well,' and he sang the tune of the first line of the National Anthem '"God *made* our gracious Queen" as much as he made you or me – and *he* knows our names – he loves us that much – we're all incredibly special to him.'

Rachel could stand it no longer. She burst into tears, and said, 'I'm sorry, I'm sorry,' over and over again. The others looked sympathetically at her, but obviously had no idea what she was sorry for. She told them in stuttering bursts with a big, noisy intake of breath between each one.

'I stole a pen (gasp) from a pencil case, (gasp) I'm sorry, I'm sorry, (gasp) I won't do it again, (gasp) I'm sorry . . .'

At the mention of a pen, Wez's and Stephen's minds were brought back to Mr Orlando's pen which they'd forgotten all about. 'Who did the pen belong to, Rachel?' said Mr Orlando quietly.

'To-Ste-phen, it-was-in-his (gasp) pen-cil case . . .' replied Rachel between sobs.

'Well, give it back to him. Stephen knows all about forgiveness, don't you Stephen – remember the Megarooney-Burgers?' But Stephen's eyes were fixed on Rachel's hand, because in it was Mr Orlando's pen, the one he had broken. How had it got into *his* pencil case?

Mr Orlando took the pen from Rachel and offered it to Stephen. 'This is yours, I believe,' he said with total sincerity.

Stephen looked at it, swallowed hard and heard himself saying, 'No,Mr Orlando, this is *yours*.'

'Why – so it is! I wondered where I'd dropped it. Thanks for being honest and returning it.'

'I didn't find it.' Now Wez was sweating (the trick was misfiring).

'Oh?' said Mr Orlando.

'No I . . .' what should he say? There was such a temptation to get his own back on Wez, and he couldn't tell a lie – oh, what a decision. ' . . . I borrowed it,' he said, truthfully '– and I'm afraid I broke it.'

'Oh, don't worry, nibs are easily replaceable. Thanks Stephen, and Rachel – you've been very brave to admit you did wrong, and say sorry. Do you know, in heaven they're having a party for both of you?' The others laughed.

'Talking of parties, Jodi, I'm terribly sorry we still haven't opened your presents. Would you mind waiting till next week?'

''Course not,' said Jodi, not minding at all. 'In fact,' she continued. 'I opened one this morning. A great T-shirt with Michael Jackson on it. It was on my front doorstep. Guess who it was from?' The others shook their heads. 'Roger Frewin.'

Adam was about to correct her, but stopped when he realised how incredible it was that Roger had brought it back.

So, someone else had also said 'sorry'.

Wez discovers how to wrap it up

Sunday 16th December

Most of the Discoverers were in their room, around a table on which were several presents – each one with a label beginning 'To Jodi . . .' There was an atmosphere of high excitement, not just because of the long awaited gift giving, but also because today they were going to sort out what they would do in the Christmas family service next week. Ideas had already begun to flow when Wez walked in sporting a new baseball jacket and trainers, which he wore with the laces undone.

'Hey you guys, like my new gear?' They mumbled noises of approval, as they always did when Wez had something new, which he seemed to most weeks.

'Steve, gimme five,' and he held up his right hand like an American Indian "How" sign. Stephen stared, not knowing what on earth Wez was talking about. Wez sighed the sort of sigh which says "I suppose I'd better show you, thicko".

'You hold your hand up like mine, then we slap them together.'

They did. Stephen did it half strength, Wez full strength, plus a bit more.

'Ow,' said Stephen, stung by the ferocity. Wez didn't want Stephen to think that he'd done him any favours by not telling Mr Orlando about his pen trick last week.

'It's not a good one unless it stings – that's what Tod says.'

'Who's Tod?' asked Susan – someone had to.

'He's this really neat guy that came back with Dad from America on business – he brought me this new gear, and taught me how to "five high" – that's what Americans call this.

'Is Tod staying with you then?' said Rachel.

Wez stopped short, then said, 'Sort of.' To get off the subject he went round to all the others doing five highs and making their palms sting. He was on Rachel when Mr Orlando walked in. Rachel heaved a sigh of relief.

'Sorry I'm late, everyone,' he said, sneaking a present on to the desk with the others.

'Mr Orlando, how are you, my man?' said Wez and held up his hand for a "five high".

Mr Orlando did the same and said, with a faultless American accent, 'All right, get down, lay some skin on me, brother.' And their hands met with a flesh melting SMACK! The others laughed – Wez secretly rubbed his throbbing hand.

'Rrrright, down to business,' Mr Orlando made a trumpet sound through tight lips. 'Happy late birthday, Jodi!' And Jodi could at last receive her presents from the others.

She got some great ones – earrings from Adam (a good replacement for the T-shirt), a Chelsea poster from Rachel and Susan, a set of crayons from Stephen, some hair slides from Deborah and a 'Snoopy' pencil case from Joel. There were only two presents left, a beautifully wrapped round one, and a scruffy old square one. She opened the round one (from Wez), taking care not to rip the lovely gold and silver paper. Inside was an old football, with muddy marks all over it.

'Thought it looked like you!' laughed Wez. Jodi flushed under her dark skin. The others didn't know what to say.

Mr Orlando put them out of their misery, 'Come on, one more left.' Jodi picked up the last one with little enthusiasm. It had no label. There was no problem tearing the paper on this one as it was very old and had probably been used several times before. Jodi's heart, which had begun to sink, suddenly did a leap. Inside was a large book called 'Favourite Recorder Tunes'. There were over a hundred tunes, and lots of wonderful colour pictures to help with understanding the music.

She looked inside the cover, and saw it was from Mr Orlando. 'Wow, thanks, this is great,' said Jodi, surprised. 'I thought, well, the wrapping, you know, er, how did you know I played the recorder?' she said.

'Oh, a little bird told me – and it just goes to show that you can't always tell what's on the inside by looking at the outside.' Mr Orlando smiled as Jodi went round thanking everyone for their presents – except Wez, who got a passing nod.

'Now to business,' said Mr Orlando, 'we have got to get on and plan for next week. We have been given about ten minutes of the service. What can we do?' There was an enormous racket, which went something like this:

'DRAMA-POETR-ITHINKWESHOULDDO-PAINTI-NO*DRAM*-WHATABOU-SINGASONG-NOWECOULDMAKEA-LETSDOAPLAY-OUCH-APAINTI-SHUTUP-GETOFF-RAMA-ONGS!!

'Whoa!' said Mr Orlando, 'One at a time. Don't forget, if we do this well it could really change things for the family services. What we need first is a theme, like we had last time when we did "Caring for the World".'

'I know,' said Adam, looking at the pile of wrapping paper in the box which they used to keep paper for recycling, 'what about presents?'

'Brilliant,' said Wez sarcastically. 'How original! Christmas presents.'

'But isn't Jesus like a present to us – from God?' said Jodi, grateful for an idea to help her best friend out and trying not to be too pleased that she had got one back on Wez.

'Excellent!' said Mr Orlando. 'A good Father's gift to the world.' The others buzzed with excitement, except Wez. 'Now, what can we do . . .' They all opened their mouths to shout, but Mr Orlando got there first, 'Hands up!' Seven hands shot up. 'Yes, Rachel?'

'We could do a big painting, like a sort of banner.'

'Yeah, like the tree me and Susan did last time,' said Jodi, holding on to Susan's arm excitedly.

'Good idea,' said Mr Orlando. Then, remembering how Rachel had been feeling last week, he said to her. 'Would you and Jodi like to do that together?' Rachel's beam was enough of an answer.

Susan began to speak, but Wez got in first. 'Won't be as good as when Susan did it, though.'

Susan had been about to say something similar – but hearing this, she changed her mind and said, 'Yes it will, Rach's brill at art – Mrs Stickley says so at school.'

'Good, now what else?' The hands were almost pulling their arms out of their sockets. 'Adam?'

'Music, we've got to do some music.'

'Great, who wants to do that?' Jodi looked at her new recorder book – she had already said a lot, maybe she ought to let someone else have a ––

'I've got a synthesizer with four hundred different sounds and fifty rhythms. My dad gave it to me for my birthday,' cut in Wez.

'Good, will you play that then?' said Mr Orlando. Wez remembered that his mother didn't like them being involved in family services and would never allow him to take it to church.

'No,' he said casually, 'I don't like playing with people who aren't as good as me.'

'Jodi, anything suitable in your book?' said Joel. Jodi was thrilled; there was a Christmas song called 'God's Gift' in the book. 'Will you be able to learn it in time?'

'It's quite long, in fact it goes over the page, but I should be all right. Oh, it's a duet, I'll need someone to play it with.' She looked at Adam.

'I'll do it,' he said, and the others groaned. More hands went up, especially one.

'Yes, Joel?'

'Please can we do some drama?'

'Yes of course, have you an idea?'

'Yes, it's about Joseph and Mary –'

Wez interrupted, and said sneeringly, 'Cor, I bet everyone will be so surprised – Joseph and Mary, wow . . .'

'It's not quite the same as normal, actually,' said Joel, thinking hard so as not to let the idea of a play vanish without trace.

'Why, do they get taken off in a space ship by ET?' Wez laughed, but no-one else did.

'No,' said Joel. An idea was forming. 'It's about . . . how Jesus looks a funny present for God to give, but really it's brilliant. Like Jodi's present from Mr Orlando *looked* awful,' he paused, but Mr Orlando's look told him he wasn't offended in the slightest, 'but really it was brill.'

'Wonderful!' said Mr Orlando, clapping his hands. Sometimes they wondered if he was any older than them. 'How many people do you need?'

'Well,' Joel counted up the people in his head, 'three should do it.' Mr Orlando considered.

'Susan, how do you fancy a starring role?' Susan did. 'And Deborah, you'd make a good Joseph, don't you think, Joel?' Joel had rather hoped he would be Joseph himself, and his face said so. 'After all, you don't want too big a part if you are going to be the director, do you?'

Joel shook his head happily, and said, 'I could type up the script on the computer at my mum's school.'

'My dad got me my own portable computer,' said Wez, 'in fact it's in my mum's car now.'

Mr Orlando carried on, 'I think we need one more thing.'

'It would be a shame not to have some poems, seeing as how people liked them last time,' said Stephen, hopefully.

'Good,' said Mr Orlando, 'we could have two – you like writing them, don't you? And Wez wrote an excellent one last time – in fact I've got it stuck on my fridge at home.' Wez felt a prickle of unease scamper up the back of his neck. He'd lost his chance to get any more of Stephen's poetry off him. If he did one himself they'd see he couldn't really write, and must have cheated before.

'Actually, I don't feel very inspired by this subject,' he said. No-one protested.

'Just you then, Stephen. And this time, you can say your poem aloud so people can hear it.'

Stephen went red at the thought. 'As long as I don't have to learn it – I've got a terrible, er . . . er . . .'

'Memory!' said Rachel. (It was a joke they had used before). Mr Orlando giggled, then said, 'Now, I think we should pray. Let's thank God for being a good father and giving us so much, then ask his help with this service.' His eyes rested on Wez, who stood up.

'I'm just going to the toilet,' he said, and left the room.

Mr Orlando prayed with the group, then set them all to work on their various tasks. When they were busy he left the room.

Outside, he found what he had expected to find, the sound of muffled crying, which stopped as soon as he approached.

'What do you want?' said Wez, angrily.

'Nothing much,' came the reply. 'Everything all right, then?'

'Course it is, just wanted to go to the toilet, that's all.' His face was away from Mr Orlando.

'So you'll be back in a minute, will you?'

'Might.'

'Hmm,' said Mr Orlando, at a loss what to say next. Then an idea came to him. 'Your mother doesn't like you being in the services, does she?' Mr Orlando thought that Wez might be trying to spoil their Christmas service preparations because of her.

'I don't care what she thinks,' he replied. 'Look, just leave me alone, will you?'

'Is that what you really want?' No answer. 'Only I got the impression that you wanted to be included.'

This surprised Wez – he thought he had done a pretty good job of trying to go it alone. 'Fat chance with that lot – they don't care about me.'

Mr Orlando looked thoughtful, 'No-one does, I suppose,' he said.

'No,' Wez said, then added after thought, 'except my dad of course.'

'Of course. And God.' Silence. Mr Orlando held his breath, the words echoed around the corridor.

'Maybe,' said Wez.

'Not maybe – God is a good father, always ready to give good things to —.'

'Stuff them!' Wez turned round in a fury. 'What's the point of presents, eh? My dad gives me presents – all the time, I've got hundreds of them. He brings me one every time he —.' Mr Orlando waited patiently. He understood now. 'All right, if you must know, my dad left ages ago – just went to work one day and never came back? OK? And now he just brings me presents every week – as if that makes it all right – but what I really want is . . . So I don't need fathers – they only let you down.' Wez's shouting was followed by a long silence. 'There, satisfied?'

When Mr Orlando spoke at last it was softly, almost a whisper. 'Wez – I always call God a *good* father – he's not like our own fathers. My dad died when I was only four – but I know that God cares for me, tons.'

'But God's miles away, just like my dad.'

'No. That's what Christmas is about. Do you know the word "Emmanuel"?'

'Course I do.'

'Well, it means "God with us". You see God's present of Jesus wasn't to make up for him not being here. Jesus *is* God – so God was coming to be with us in the only way he could, as a human being. God was present, *in* his present.' Wez looked thoughtful.

'Some people can be a bit like our presents to Jodi this morning. Some look very nice on the outside, with big polite smiles, just like the best wrapping paper. But inside they can be horrible – like your present this morning. And sometimes they appear grotsville outside, but inside they just want to be . . . included.'

'Which am I, then?' asked Wez at length

'Well, Wez, only you can choose – it's your decision and no-one else's, isn't it?'

And Mr Orlando turned and went back into the room.

The others were excitedly getting ready. Joel, Deborah and Susan were arguing over something to do with the play they were making up. Jodi and Rachel had started to make a huge banner. Stephen was reading the Christmas story in the Bible to get some ideas, and Adam was trying to learn 'God's Gift' on an old recorder he'd found. Wez came back in, with blotchy eyes – and everything stopped. No-one said a word, except Mr Orlando.

'Now, I've had an idea. Things will go more smoothly if we have someone to be responsible for the whole exercise – what they call a "supremo".'

'I think it should be Joel,' said Jodi. Everyone agreed, and there was much enthusiastic discussion.

'What about Wez?' said Rachel, innocent as a butterfly, "He's not doing anything yet.' The group's enthusiasm suddenly vanished like a television set being switched off. Mr Orlando was quick as ever.

'Excellent,' he said, 'Wez will be the stage manager, the one who makes sure everyone has what they need. You can use your computer to make neat copies of everyone's words and a running order. You and Joel can work together, OK?' The others froze, fearing another burst of insults from Wez.

'Yes, all right, Mr Orlando – as long as Joel doesn't mind me using my computer and not his mum's.' You could have bowled the Discoverers over with a Christmas tree bauble.

'I don't know what Mr Orlando said to him,' whispered Deborah to Susan, 'but it certainly did the trick.'

They all carried on with their preparations.

After a while, Mr Orlando slapped the table, 'Rrrright – time for today's game, what shall we play?' There was no answer – the Discoverers were much too busy to think about games. Eventually it *was* time to stop.

'Now, we'll meet slightly early next week again to have a run through, OK?' They nodded. 'Good – see you then. Have a nice day!' They filed out. Wez, the last to leave, gave Mr Orlando a stinging 'five high'. With his new clothes, he looked a bit like a nicely wrapped present – perhaps too nice. The question was, what was going on inside? But that was up to Wez – Mr Orlando hoped for the best.

Wez closed the door behind him and walked, almost skipped, along the corridor. Now, he thought, I'll need some glue, scissors, cotton wool, a heavy weight – and my book of practical jokes, of course . . .

Joel's role

Sunday 23rd December

It wasn't cold enough for December, just like the woman on the BBC weather forecast had said. The mean, grey clouds only promised the misery of drizzle rather than the icy tingle that told you snow was in the air. Even the wind was calm.

There was, however, one place that wasn't calm – Joel's head. He had slept only a couple of hours last night because of thinking about today. Both his mum and Wez had helped get things ready all week, and now the day had arrived – aargh!

The Discoverers were frantically practising their pieces when Mr Orlando came in. They froze in their positions hoping they wouldn't be asked to sit down because they were *much* too busy.

'Good morning, everyone,' he said cheerfully, as if there was nothing special happening. Seven and a half pairs of anxious eyes greeted him (Rachel had just got something in one eye, so it was closed). 'All ready, are we?' They started to talk at once.

Mr Orlando sympathised. 'Yes, yes – I'm nervous too, but it will be all right.'

'We just have to trust God, don't we, Mr Orlando,' said Wez, too politely.

'Absolutely right,' said Mr Orlando. 'Now then, Joel, you're in charge.'

'OK, er, everyone grab what you need.' They all obeyed at once, scuttling about the room. 'Rrrright,' Joel went on, imitating Mr Orlando, who laughed, 'we'll see the painting first.'

Rachel and Jodi shuffled forward with their large banner. It was painted on two sides of an enormous box, cut up so they were flat – and was fantastic. The night sky stretched over a dark valley in which sat the little town of Bethlehem. Above it was the most beautiful star, a delight of gold and silver with glitter stuck on it.

Mr Orlando was the first to speak. 'That's fantastic, you two,'

'My dad helped us, he does art at night school,' said Jodi proudly.

'And I did the star,' added Rachel – Jodi looked at her – 'well most of it anyway.'

'We'd better get it to the church as quickly as possible. I've checked with Nick the curate, and he's going to hang it behind that platform where everyone can see it. It'll be like scenery.'

'I'll take it over,' said Wez. 'That's what a stage manager does, isn't it?'

'I'll help,' said Adam.

'No, it's OK – it's not far, and you need to practise.' And Wez picked it up carefully, and left.

'I thought we'd have the music first,' said Joel.

Jodi and Adam began their recorder duet. It sounded just right, although there was a slight pause to turn over the page in the middle. They finished just as Wez came in.

'That was quick,' said Mr Orlando.

'I don't hang about,' he replied – and it was then that Mr Orlando noticed how bulgy his pockets were. Wez cleared away the music stand and the book, and took the recorders from the two players.

'Right, drama next,' Joel announced. 'Have you got all the bits and pieces my mum gave us, Wez?'

'They're called "props", and they're here. Cradle, straw to go in it, false beard, three dressing gowns, two tea towels, long wig, beach ball for Mary's bump (Rachel giggled), doll for the baby Jesus and a torch.'

The three actors went through the sketch, and remembered most of it. Mary (Susan) and Joseph (Deborah) arrived at the inn and Joseph said, 'Innkeeper, a room for my wife who is great with child.'

Then came Joel's favourite line – he said, 'You want a room? The answer begins with an "N" and rhymes with "go".'

To which Mary said, 'No? Oh dear, what are we to do?' They were then shown the stable.

Joseph had a speech whilst Mary 'had' the baby, which meant going off stage and quickly taking out the beach ball. Meanwhile Joel did a quick change into his shepherd's costume with Wez's help. Mary came back on with the cradle to show that the scene had changed to inside the stable – and said, 'Later that night'.

Joel then came into the stable as a shepherd and told everyone how he'd first seen an angel and now, the baby Jesus.

'This is the best bit,' said Joel with great excitement, 'whilst the audience are —'

'Actually, Joel,' said Mr Orlando respectfully, 'in church it's probably better to call them a congregation.' The others smiled.

'Yeah well, whilst . . . everyone is listening to my speech, Wez puts a torch in the cradle and it looks like the glow you see round Jesus' head in pictures, to show that he is God.'

'I like it!' said Mr Orlando, 'and so will the audience.'

'Congregation!' they all shouted at once.

'Quite right, and then it's Stephen, isn't it?'

'Yes, my poem's called "Shepherd's Tale".'

'Shepherds don't have tails!' said Rachel, to much giggling.

'No, tale like in a story, shall I read it?' He did, in a funny sort of voice. 'My brother helped a bit, but the joke is mine.'

Joel worried that it was a bit like his shepherd's speech – he should have warned Stephen. But Mr Orlando said, 'Excellent poem – though I think that you'd better not say "pooey and smelly".'

'But it was a stable,' said Stephen, quite correctly.

'How about using "mucky"?' said Mr Orlando.
·OK – I'll quickly change it.'

'Stephen, what does "stonking" mean?' asked Susan.

'I'm not sure, I just like the sound of it. My dad's from Yorkshire, and he says it. He reckons all the best shepherds are from Yorkshire, that's why I did it in a Yorkshire accent.'

'Good,' said Mr Orlando, 'now we need to get going or they'll start without us.' He noticed Joel and said, 'Right – pray!' They all closed their eyes, except Wez.

'Dear Lord Jesus – thanks that we can celebrate your birthday every year. Thanks that you're the best present ever. Help us to do our best for you – and please help people to enjoy the service, Amen.' They started to pick up their props. Mr Orlando went over to Joel, who was looking a bit worried.

'Look,' said Mr Orlando, 'you've done all you can, Joel – we've got to trust Jesus now. In God's hands even a smelly old stable produced someone wonderful, so think what he can do through your efforts. *Trust*, Joel.' Joel nodded, realising that Mr Orlando trusted *him*.

Wez was collecting things together, and soon they were all ready to go. They had to run quickly to the church as it was raining gently. They got in and took their things to the front.

'Oh no!' said Rachel, 'Look!' They all looked up at the banner. It was in the right place, but it had specks of faded colour all over it, and the paint on the star had run so that there was a silver stripe right down into the top of the Bethlehem.

'Yes, I found it outside in the rain,' said Nick the curate, coming out of the vestry, 'I don't think anyone will notice.'

'Wasn't my fault the church was locked,' said Wez. 'Come on.' In the busyness, the banner was soon forgotten, except by Jodi and Rachel who looked up at it and said nothing.

St Margaret's was an oldish church which still had

fairly high pews. So in order that people could see what was going on, there was a big, carpeted wooden platform at the front. The Discoverers sat in a special pew just behind it so they could get on and off the platform without much fuss.

The service began. No-one had ever seen the church so full. The Discoverers looked at the congregation, spotting their parents and friends who had come to see them. Jodi thought she caught a glimpse of Roger Frewin, though she wasn't sure. At the end of each pew was a tall holder with a lighted candle in it. The Christmas tree looked wonderful with its coloured lights, and there were loads of holly sprigs all over the place.

Things went very quickly, and it wasn't long before they heard Reverend Wibble say, 'And now, we are *very* fortunate to have the Discoverers to show us some *things* they've been working on.' He sat down.

Wez put a screwdriver and a tube of glue back in his pocket and took the music stand and music book on to the platform followed by Jodi and Adam. He gave the book to Jodi and hurried back to his seat. Jodi put the book on the stand; after a wobble and a creak, it collapsed. She recovered the book from the lap of an elderly woman in the front row whilst Adam fiddled with the stand. He just couldn't get it to work. In the end, after what seemed like hours, Joel appeared and said he'd hold the book for them. Adam then realised he'd left his recorder in the pew – but Wez brought it up, after putting some cotton wool back in his pocket.

Eventually they started. To begin with, it sounded wonderful – they had practised hard on three evenings that week. But all of a sudden things started to go wrong. Adam's recorder didn't seem to want to play all the notes he wanted it to. There was cotton wool in the thumb hole (although he didn't know this) which meant that he couldn't play any notes which should have that hole open.

As a result, every so often there was a terrible clash

of notes. They played on not knowing what to do, then Joel went to turn the page over and found it stuck to the next one. Fortunately, he had the presence of mind to yank them apart in time, though it ripped the paper. After a while, Adam gave up his part and sang the words, so it finished up sounding not too bad, though they were convinced it was awful.

Mr Orlando stood up to give a short link into the drama. Joel was supposed to have been getting changed all this time, but because he'd held the music, he was late. Wez put a pin back in his pocket, and then gave Susan the beach ball to stuff up her jumper to make it look as if she was pregnant. He stuck Deborah's beard on her face, and left them to put on their dressing gown coats.

Joel was next. Wez said to him, 'Here, put the wig on, you'll have to take your glasses off first.' He took Joel's glasses and placed them on the floor. 'Your coat is on the pew behind you,' he said. Joel without his glasses was like a mole in daylight. He fumbled around for his coat, then *crunch*! Joel picked up his glasses from the floor, one lens smashed, the other missing.

'Oh no, trust me,' he said, 'I'll never be able to act now. I'll keep falling off the stage.' Mr Orlando had finished his introduction and Deborah and Susan were saying their first lines.

'Give the wig to me,' said Wez. 'I learnt the script whilst I was typing it into my computer – I'll do the part.' Joel had no choice but to give him the costume.

The drama was progressing well when it came to the inn scene. 'Innkeeper, a room for my wife who is pregnant,' said Deborah, as Joseph.

'You want a room?' began Wez, 'well the answer begins with a "Y" and rhymes with "guess".' Susan and Deborah stared open mouthed, completely at a loss – the people in the congregation started to giggle. Susan just said,

'Oh dear, what are we to do?' (And she meant it).

Wez continued, 'We've got loads of rooms, come in – would you like one with a shower?' The congregation were now laughing quite loudly. Susan and Deborah were near to tears. Wez was just about to say his next line about Mary needing to go on a diet, when he was aware of a presence behind him.

'Please excuse my son,' said Mr Orlando's voice in a Yorkshire accent, 'he's always trying to make money – fancy promising rooms we haven't got. Go away and clean the cellar.' And he shoved Wez off the stage. 'Sorry, but we have *no* rooms.'

Susan was relieved that she could now say her proper line, 'No? Oh dear, what are we to do?'

'I have a stable, here let me show you,' continued Mr Orlando and led them to the back of the stage where the cradle was. He left as Deborah began her next speech. Susan went off stage to take out the beach ball, but as she did so it went down, making a loud noise which sounded like a huge 'raspberry'.

Deborah was quick, 'Naughty cattle,' she said. Then whilst the congregation giggled, her beard fell off.

Joel could sense what was going on. Would Wez know about the shepherd's part? Would he get the lines wrong like he had as the innkeeper? In desperation he prayed simply, 'Lord Jesus, help me.'

He fumbled for his shepherd's costume and bumped into Stephen. Of course! 'Stephen,' whispered Joel, 'grab this coat and get on – you're the shepherd.'

'But I don't know the lines,' panicked Stephen.

'Say your poem – it's about the same thing – just get on!'

'But Wez is looking after it for me.'

Joel, having found the unbroken lens, looked through it and saw the poem on the pew where Wez had been sitting. He pushed the poem into Stephen's hand, then pushed him on to the stage. Wez, meanwhile, *was* ready to play the shepherd. He had already prepared his opening lines, which started, 'Angel! I never saw no angel –

and if they are *wise* men, why didn't they come by car?' But first, he had to put the torch in the cradle. He put in *a* torch, and put the matches back in his pocket. It was then that he saw Stephen rocketted on to the stage. The cue line came and Stephen, unfolding his paper, began in his best Yorkshire accent,

'We was out on the hillside, minding our sheep,
Not even a wolf to concern us.
It were colder than freezing and all of us wished
That someone would invent the Thermos. (laughter)

'Then suddenly something fantastical happened,
I tell you for nowt I were frightened.
The sky turned from black, to brilliant white,
Like in 't' morning when your mum turns the light on.

'There were thousands of angels, all singing their heads off,
One sheep near jumped out of its fleece.
They told us to go to a tiny poor stable,
To worship the Prince of Peace.

'So off I did trot, with a lamb as a pressie,
And saw a stonking good thing.
Though mucky and smelly, it were beautiful, holy,
To be there at the birth of a King.'

One more verse to go, thought Stephen as he turned the page over. He froze in horror. The last verse had been completely scribbled over – he couldn't read a single word. He paused, the congregation waited, Joel prayed again, the cradle seemed to glow more brightly and Susan and Deborah started to feel hot. Stephen's memory clicked into gear.

'It was just so amazing to be there in the stable,
And Mary looked up and we knew,
That God had now given the best ever present,
To us scruffy shepherds and you.'

The congregation then did something amazing – they clapped. In church! And as if beaming with pride, Susan and Deborah glowed more brightly.

Suddenly Adam shouted, 'The cradle's on fire!' Wez had used one of the candles as a torch, and the straw had caught alight. Before anyone could move, Joel, still squinting through his lens, grabbed the jug of water they'd had in their pew and threw it at the fire. However, only having one good eye, he missed and it went all over Wez, who was still sitting behind the cradle. Eventually, Mr Orlando saved the day with a fire blanket. The service continued, but not even Nick's puppet in the sermon could top that.

Afterwards, when the others were cleaning up, Mr Orlando went up to Joel, who was sitting in a pew – alone.

'But we prayed, and it went wrong!'

'Joel,' said Mr Orlando, 'remember God can bring good out of even the worst things. And anyway, the congregation seemed to thoroughly enjoy it – that was a brilliant idea to get Stephen to go on as the shepherd. It worked really well.' Joel smiled.

'Look, God's given us all the freedom to do good things and bad. If someone chooses to do nasty things, they will happen. If God sorted everything out perfectly all the time, there'd be nothing left to discover, we'd all be perfect – and bored stiff.'

Reverend Wibble came up. 'Well done Discoverers,' he said as they assembled – minus Wez who had been driven home by his angry mother to dry off.

'Did the audience, er, congregation enjoy it?' said Joel.

'To *most* people you went down like a *house* on fire.' They laughed when they realised what he'd said. 'The banner was *splendid* – such a good idea to show the *light* from the star reaching into the stable, like God's *hand* delivering his gift to us. And that tune is one of my *favourites* – you don't often hear the words. And as for the innkeeper's son – *brilliant* idea. The whole thing was absolutely *stonking!*' The Discoverers grinned. 'Joel, I believe you held the *whole* thing together?' Joel half nodded.

'How I wish family services could be always this much *fun* – it's just that some people . . .' His voice trailed off.

'We'll pray about it,' said Mr Orlando.

'And trust Jesus,' said Joel.

'Good stuff!' said Reverend Wibble. And he walked off saying, 'Merry Christmas.'

And it certainly was.

To begin at the end . . .

Sunday 30th December

As Mr Orlando stood outside the door of the Discoverers room listening to the sound of cheering inside, he wondered if they had realised it was his last week. Reverend Wibble had said he'd be there until the end of the year, and that time had now come.

When he entered, he saw the group cheering on Susan, who had a black box in her hand with a large aerial sticking out of it. They had each brought a Christmas present in, and this was Adam's remote controlled tank. They were all having turns at racing it around the room.

'When's my turn?' he said. Susan completed the course, then handed him the control box.

'You have to go round all the tables, then climb the ramp over the waste paper bin,' Adam began.

'Is that all?' said Mr Orlando, 'Baby's game!'

'*And*,' continued Rachel, 'beat the record time of forty three seconds.'

'Ah!' Mr Orlando was slightly less confident. 'Oh well, say go.'

'Go!' said Deborah, who was the official timer with *her* Christmas present – a new watch. Mr Orlando did a lot better than they expected, but still came in at just over a minute.

'Well done, Stephen, you win,' said Deborah. Stephen smiled.

'Rrrright, sit down you rrrrrabble!' They all found their places and settled down to see what would happen today. There was an empty place.

'Where's Wez?' They looked around. For the first time they realised that he wasn't there and, to be honest, they weren't too upset. They had all found it difficult last week. Each had suspicions about who had made things go wrong during their presentation, though none of them knew exactly. 'Anyway, we must carry on,' said Mr Orlando, with a hint of sadness.

They looked down at their tables. The sudden thought of Wez, and the memory of last Sunday (which Christmas had forced from their minds) reduced them to a mood like the one you get on the last day of a long-looked-forward-to-holiday. Mr Orlando saw this at once, and knew that a story was called for. He thought hard. It had to be a good one.

'How many Wise Men were there at the birth of Jesus?' he said.

They wondered what he was on about. Usually his questions were a little more difficult than this.

'Three of course,' said Adam.

'Where does it say that?' said Mr Orlando. They looked in their Bibles and saw that it didn't. 'Surprise!' he continued. 'There could have been three, but who knows? What colour coat did Jesus wear?'

'White,' said Rachel.

'Where does it say that?'

'It's in that picture on the wall.' Their eyes followed her finger, pointing to the old picture of Jesus carrying a lamb.

'Yes, but he could have worn any colour, even stripes, I think they were "in" then.' He looked at Joel, who was wearing a new striped jumper – they all giggled.

'You see, the Bible tells us some things, but leaves out others. So it's sometimes fun to guess what the other things were. For example, who was Izzy Barzak?' They shook their heads. 'He was the boy with the lunch at the feeding of the five thousand.'

'Was he?' asked Jodi, thumbing through her new Bible.

'Well, he might have been. Let's pretend he was. I mean *someone* had to have the lunch, so it might as well have been him. Let's also pretend that his father was

. . . a dustman – called Zak. Heard the joke about the dustbin? It's a load of rubbish.' They all groaned.

'Anyway,' continued Mr Orlando, 'one day they decided to go on a picnic. Mrs Zak knew this was a problem, because her husband had a humongous appetite. Last time they had been for one, she had packed everything but the kitchen sink. He was so hungry that when they got back he'd eaten that as well.

'She asked Izzy and his sister Lizzy what they wanted to eat. 'Fish paste sarnies,' they answered. So she picked up five small loaves and two fishes. She thought if she made them now, they would go all soggy. So she packed them in her husband's large dustbin-shaped lunch box. She also put in his mackintosh which was made out of a dustbin liner for them to sit on. It was Zak's packed black plastic mac.

'Izzy took his new cheetapult with him.'

'What's that?' asked Stephen.

'It's like a catapult only a bit more powerful. Lizzy wanted a turn, but I'm afraid that Izzy was not like our Adam was with his tank. He didn't like sharing, and snatched it out of her grasp. Lizzy thumped him on the arm, and just as he was about to hit her back, Mrs Zak shouted, "Listen you two, if there's any more of this arguing you'll stay at home."

"But he won't let me play with his cheetapult," protested Lizzy.

"When will you learn that you've got to share, Izz?" she said, taking the toy from him. "To teach you a lesson, you can carry the lunch." And the dustbin with the food in it was thrust into his hands.

'They walked on a bit further and saw a huge crowd sitting on the side of a hill.

"Hey, you know who they're listening to, don't you?" said Zak. The others shook their heads. "It's Jesus!"

"Jesus who?" said Mrs Zak.

"Jesus who heals people and raises them from the dead," said Zak a little impatiently.

"Oh, *that* Jesus?"

"YEAH!!!!!!!" said Zak, his eyes as big as dinner plates.

"Well, we'd better sit down and have a listen. Izzy, put the food in the cool box."

"But I can't, Mum," he answered, "they haven't been invented yet."

"Well do the best you can then, and stop making excuses,' she said sitting down. Izzy took the food out of the dustbin-shaped lunch box and left.

'He picked his way among the people to a tree, climbed it and left the food there in a cool breeze. He could also see Jesus better from there.

'Before long, he was laughing like everyone else. It's easy to think that listening to Jesus was dull and quiet, but it wasn't. Just think, there were over five thousand people listening for hours – so he must have been very entertaining. In fact at this moment he was telling a story about how a tax collector, who everyone really hated, had had his prayer answered and a Pharisee, had not. So the gales of laughter were enough to make a dustbin flip its lid.

'At the front of the crowd, Peter was wiping tears of laughter from his eyes with the back of his hand. Then Jesus called him over.

"Peter, we've got a slight problem."

"It's never seemed to worry you in the past, Master."

"I've kept these people here since breakfast, so they haven't got any lunch with them. I can't send them off to buy any, I've got loads more important things to say to them. Judas, how much money have we got?"

"About, er, two pounds fifty."

"Oh, not quite enough," said Jesus. Then he spotted Izzy. "Peter, go and ask that boy if we can borrow his lunch."

"Which one?"

"That one there – in the tree, just to the left of the group of people doing a dance." Peter shot off.

'Meanwhile, back at the Zak's, Zak said, "All that laughing's made me hungry enough to eat a donkey – when's lunch?"
"As soon as I can spot Izzy," replied his wife looking around. "Listen to that rumbling, sounds like thunder – good job I brought your mac, Zak." She then realised that the thunder was really the sound of five thousand rumbly tummies. "No-one else seems to have brought any grub – good job we did." Just then, Izzy came back.

He looked a bit sheepish as he said, "Mum, you know what you said about sharing – well, I think we, er, really ought to share our lunch."

"Rubbish, there's hardly enough for us – and anyway, I bought that fish specially. Come on, give it here."

"I can't," he stammered. "You see, I gave it away."

"You did what?!" said Zak, Mrs Zak and Lizzy together. "This man said that Jesus wanted to borrow it, and I thought you wouldn't mind and —" But before he could say any more, Zak had picked him up, put him in the dustbin and sat on it.

'Just then, they noticed that some men were giving food to everyone. The Zaks were right on the edge of the crowd, so it was a while before one of the disciples (it was Peter, though they didn't know this) gave them some. To their amazement, it was exactly the same as what they'd brought, only this time they had five loaves and two fishes *each*.

"Mind if I borrow this?" said Peter, picking up the dustbin. "Jesus wants to use it." Zak, his mouth bulging with fish sarnie, couldn't answer before Peter had hoisted it on to his shoulder and left.

'Izzy had fallen asleep, so the first he knew of this was when the lid was taken off, and a kind face he sort of recognised peered in.

"What have we here?" It was Jesus. "Ah, it's Izzy from the tree – come on, let's help you out." He did. "Thanks so much for sharing your lunch with me and my friends."

"What friends?" said Izzy stretching his legs.

"These!" said Jesus, indicating the whole hillside full of munching people.

"Wow!" said Izzy, and looked at the lunch that Peter offered him.

"Thanks for the food, Jesus!"

"Best grace I ever heard," said Jesus, watching Izzy eat.

'Izzy arrived back to his family on the top of the dustbin, carried by three disciples. When they'd gone, Zak said, "Three blokes to carry one bin and a boy? They must be weedy wet-legs," and he tried to lift the bin. His face went redder and redder till Mrs Zak thought he'd burst a gasket. He lifted the lid, "What's in here —?"

He stared, and Mrs Barzak stared, and Lizzy stared, and Izzy laughed and said, "There's enough leftovers in there to keep us going for months!"

"Well," replied Zak, patting his stomach, "a couple of days anyway." The end,' said Mr Orlando, sitting back.

The Discoverers clapped.

'What it really like that?' said Rachel.

'I doubt it,' said Mr Orlando, 'but it was fun to imagine, wasn't it? It's so easy to think of Jesus as being boring – but he wasn't – far from it! And of course the story had the same meaning – and that's the important thing.'

Mr Orlando sat back in his chair. 'Remember I asked you ages ago what you had discovered?' They nodded. 'Well, I'm going to ask you again now. What have you discovered from that story?' They thought.

'To share with people,' said Rachel.

'To obey Jesus,' said Susan.

'That Jesus thinks you're important even if you're small and in a crowd of five thousand people,' said Stephen with a grin.

'To trust him,' said Joel, 'like Izzy did.'

'Yes, even if it seems like the pits, Jesus is there and will bring good out of it somehow, if we trust him – just like we are doing for the family services, eh, Joel? Remember, Jesus died – which was awful, terrible – *but* there was a glorious resurrection. Good,' he continued, 'all of those things. And that's what I've discovered too.'

'Didn't you know them already?' asked Deborah.

'Oh yes, but you learn things over and over again with Jesus. You see he never stops surprising you.'

'How did *you* discover them?' asked Jodi.

'Well, Jodi, I discovered them through all of you.' They stared.

'Surprised?' They nodded. 'And that includes Wez. You see, you're never too old to learn. You have your part to play in God's world as much as anyone – I sometimes think we grown-ups need to listen to people your age a lot more.' And they remembered for the first time in weeks that he was actually very grown up.

At that moment Reverend Wibble burst in.

'Come on Discoverers, some of your *parents* are waiting.' They hadn't realised what the time was. 'Before you go, I have a couple of *announcements* to make. Firstly, Wez has left *Discoverers.* He and his mother have gone to live in another part of the *country.*' The Discoverers felt they ought to be glad at this news – but deep down the thought of Wez leaving like that made them quite sad.

Mr Orlando felt it too, but was able to say, 'Does that mean that you are free to accept new ideas into the family services?'

'Well, yes, I suppose it *does* – but some people seem so happy to criticize, without giving any positive *ideas*,' replied Reverend Wibble.

'I think this bunch may have some,' said Mr Orlando.

For the next five minutes the vicar of St Margarets, East Hanworth was bombarded with countless ideas for things they would love to see, hear and do in family services – most based on what they had discovered over the past few weeks.

'Such a joy to have ideas and *enthusiasm*,' said Reverend Wibble with a wobble, genuinely overcome.

'And Mr Orlando will always have more!' said Rachel, to the cheers of the others.

'Oh, but he won't,' said Reverend Wibble. 'I thought you *knew*. Their faces were frozen in a mixture of shock and dread. 'Today's his last day. Don't you remember I said he was with us until the end of the *year*?' Now, they did.

They turned to Mr Orlando, but he had gone. No-one had noticed him slip quietly away during their splurge of ideas. Reverend Wibble, aware of something in the atmosphere but not really knowing what – except that there was a lot of it, simply said, "Er, well, don't be too long – last one out turn off the *light* – and, er, Happy New *Year*. Yes . . .' He left.

They were like statues. It was a full minute before anyone moved. It was Jodi who had seen a note on Mr Orlando's table. She opened it, read it, then her arm dropped slowly fall to her side. Adam took it and read it aloud.

'Dear Discoverers,

I'm not very good at "goodbyes", I'm afraid. My time with you is up – for now. I do hope I'll be able to come and see you again some time – but anyway, I'll see you in heaven if not before. I've enjoyed our times together very, very much. I am sorry about Wez. Look after Reverend Wibble and remember, Jesus never runs out of surprises.

Keep discovering!

Your friend,

Orlando.'

They left the room. Happy New Year? How could they be happy again? Yet as they walked slowly, silently down the corridor, it was almost as if Mr Orlando was still with them. And even though they were sad, there was a strange sort of hope – like a caterpillar must feel just before it turns into a butterfly. Maybe Jesus hadn't run out of surprises. Ah, but that would be another story.